MEDITERRANEAN DOCTORS

Let these exotic doctors sweep you off your feet...

Be tantalised by their smouldering good-looks,
romanced by their fiery passion,
and warmed by the emotional power
of these strong and caring men...

MEDITERRANEAN DOCTORS

Passionate about life, love and medicine

Alison Roberts lives in Christchurch, New Zealand. She began her working career as a primary school teacher, but now juggles available working hours between writing and active duty as an ambulance officer. Throwing in a large dose of parenting, housework, gardening and pet-minding keeps life busy, and teenage daughter Becky is responsible for an increasing number of days spent on equestrian pursuits. Finding time for everything can be a challenge, but the rewards make the effort more than worthwhile.

Recent titles by the same author:

MARRYING THE MILLIONAIRE DOCTOR*
HER FOUR-YEAR BABY SECRET
THE ITALIAN SURGEON CLAIMS HIS BRIDE
CHRISTMAS BRIDE-TO-BE
THE PLAYBOY DOCTOR'S PROPSAL*

*Crocodile Creek

THE ITALIAN SURGEON'S CHRISTMAS MIRACLE

BY
ALISON ROBERTS

MILLS & BOON®
Pure reading pleasure™

First published in Great Britain 2008
Harlequin Mills & Boon Limited,
Eton House, 18-24 Paradise Road, Richmond, Surrey TW9 1SR

© Alison Roberts 2008

ISBN: 978 0 263 19916 1

Set in Times Roman 10½ on 12¾ pt
15-1008-48104

Printed and bound in Great Britain
by Antony Rowe Ltd, Chippenham, Wiltshire

THE ITALIAN SURGEON'S CHRISTMAS MIRACLE

CHAPTER ONE

THE silly season.

Aptly named.

And the sooner it was over the better, as far as Luke Harrington was concerned.

Chaos was gaining hold in the cardiology ward of St Elizabeth's Children's Hospital and the people who should be at least trying to keep a lid on things were clearly failing.

The noise level was well above normal, thanks to children already being hyped up by the approach of Christmas Day. There seemed to be a lot of giggling going on and the seasonal music had somehow followed him from the theatre suite. Gaudy decorations hung everywhere, including loops of fat silver tinsel on doorframes that threatened to garrotte anyone in his position of being over six feet in height.

A nurse passed him, a small child balanced on her hip, a huge white teddy bear under her other arm. The bear was wearing a Santa hat and the nurse was singing 'Jingle Bells'. The child was beating time with two small fists and a wide grin on her face. Luke smiled back.

'Hello, Bella. I'm coming to see you soon.'

'Three sleeps,' Bella informed him. 'Mummy says I'll be

home by then but even if I'm not, Father Christmas will know where to find me.'

'He sure will.' Bella's nurse had stopped singing. 'Let's get you back to bed, Trouble, so Mr *Harrington* will know where to find you.' The tone suggested that this nurse was well aware of the problems caused recently by his patients being anywhere but in their beds when Luke did his rounds.

The charge nurse, Margaret, had spotted his approach to the central nurses' station. She held out a clipboard.

'Can you sign, please, Luke? It's the telephone order you gave for increased analgesia for Daniel.'

Luke reached for a pen. 'Have the results come in on Baby Harris?'

'Yes. I've got them right here for you.' Margaret turned as swiftly as her substantial figure allowed, reaching for a manila folder on the cluttered desk.

Luke scrawled his name, looked up to wait for the folder but then found his attention diverted to the same place Margaret's had been. A large artificial Christmas tree had been positioned near the central desk. Cardboard boxes were scattered around its base. A nurse was kneeling beside one of the boxes and she had a group of children gathered around her. As she opened the box, the children grabbed decorations and that was what had attracted Margaret's notice.

'Not those ones, Ange.' She moved to pick up the box. 'I thought we'd got rid of these. We've got all the lovely new decorations for this year, remember?'

More boxes were opened to reveal decorations still wrapped in tissue paper. The box that was overflowing with rather sad-looking, bent, cardboard stars and chipped coloured balls was pushed into a corner behind Luke, near the rubbish bin. Margaret straightened and smiled at Luke's expression as he watched children gleefully shredding tissue paper and crowing delightedly over their discoveries.

'It's Christmas.' No one else would get away with the kind of motherly rebukes Margaret could deliver. 'We're allowed a little bit of mess.' She handed him the manila folder.

Luke said nothing. Margaret had been running this ward for ever. She knew as well as he did why tidiness was important. Right now it would be impossible to move a bed past this section of the corridor. The boxes were enough of an obstacle course for people, let alone, say, a crash trolley. Yes, it was highly unlikely that an emergency would occur in the next fifteen minutes but what if it did? Part of Luke's not inconsiderable skill as a surgeon came from being able to anticipate and prevent a broken link in a chain of response.

He placed the folder on the desk and opened it just as his pager sounded again. Automatically, he reached for the nearby phone.

'Harrington.'

'It's an outside call, Mr Harrington. From a Mr Battersby. He's been waiting a while. Shall I put it through?'

Luke was very tempted to say he didn't have time to take this call, but he thought better of it. It wasn't just the chaos of the run-up to Christmas that he wanted to be over. 'Put him on,' he said. 'Thank you.'

His solicitor obviously respected time constraints. He got straight to the point.

'Sorry to disturb you, Mr Harrington, but we have a problem.'

'Oh?' Luke tucked the phone between a shrugged shoulder and his ear as he opened the folder and fanned out the sheaf of test results with one hand.

'Have you, by any chance, had the opportunity to take a look at this house on Sullivan Avenue that you've inherited?'

Maybe the constraints weren't understood clearly enough.

'Time is a luxury in my line of business, Mr Battersby.' Luke frowned at the graph in front of him. Started at birth, continued by the GP and now being monitored by ward staff, charting the weight of a three-week-old boy who had been admitted two days ago in urgent need of major heart surgery.

'Oh, I understand that. But…'

A muscle in Luke's jaw bunched. As many of the staff at Lizzies were aware, '*but*' was one of his least favourite words. 'Find a solution, not an excuse' was a phrase he had to use all too often.

His tone was still patient, however. Calm and professional. What any member of the public might expect to hear from the head of the paediatric cardiothoracic surgical department.

'We've been through this, Mr Battersby,' he said. 'The house is derelict. It's sitting on a particularly valuable piece of real estate.' And central London real estate was always valuable. Especially this close to Regent's Park. Luke raised his gaze for a moment. If he walked past the Christmas tree into one of the inpatient rooms on that side of the ward, he could probably see the property from the height the second floor of the hospital provided.

Not that he would recognise the house. He hadn't seen it and he didn't intend to.

'Extremely valuable,' the solicitor concurred.

Luke ignored the murmur. 'As I told you last week, I want the house gone. Demolished.'

Wiped from the face of the earth.

'And I want it done immediately.' Luke allowed his determination to show. 'I want a clean piece of land to put on the market in the new year. Preferably the first of January.'

Good. The baby's weight was creeping up again, finally.

Having dropped to 1.6 kg due to an inability to feed, the underlying heart condition and a respiratory infection, it was now back to 2 kg. An acceptable point to go ahead with the surgery.

'We have a problem with that,' the annoying voice in his ear repeated. 'Particularly the time frame.'

'I'm not interested in problems.' Luke caught the phone with his hand, preparing to end the call. 'That's why I employ a firm with the kind of reputation Battersby, Battersby and Gosling has. You sort it.'

'It's not that simple.'

Nothing ever was. Luke was doing a quick mental re-arrangement of his commitments. Which of tomorrow morning's cases could be shuffled? Some might well have to wait an extra day or two given the length of time this case would involve and nobody would be happy about that. Not that anyone was going to get out of the intensive care unit let alone get home for Christmas with surgery planned for tomorrow, but everybody wanted it over with and recuperation to look forward to. Christmas was a family celebration tiny Liam Harris might never be able to share if this surgery didn't happen very quickly.

'It's the tenants, you see…'

'What?' Theatre schedules slid to the back of Luke's mind. He tried to block out the increasing noise level from the excited children helping to decorate the tree. 'What do you mean, "tenants"? According to the information you sent me, there's been no income on this property since its owner died.'

'It's complicated. There's been an informal arrangement, apparently. Your father—'

Already tense muscles tightened another notch. Luke's jaw ached. 'Giovanni Moretti is no relative of mine.'

The name might be on his birth certificate but it had never been spoken. Or used. Part of his genetic make-up, admittedly, but it had been buried long ago as something to be ashamed of. Despised.

Italian.

Emotional.

The path to chaos and misery and broken lives.

All so far in the past even the reminder had been shocking, but Luke had been well brought up. Given strength of character like tempered steel. He knew not to go there. Not to even take a single step in that direction. He could almost see his grandmother's approving nod as he drew in a careful breath.

'Proceed with the demolition,' he ordered calmly. 'The tenants will simply have to find somewhere else to squat.'

'They can't.' Mr Battersby, senior, sounded a lot less frail than Luke knew him to be. Defiant, even.

'Excuse me?'

'There's children involved.' Reginald Battersby cleared his throat and his tone became slightly bemused. 'Rather a lot of them, actually. And they're in the care of a young woman who flatly refuses to leave the house before Christmas. She is somewhat…ah…passionate about it.'

Passion. Even the word was distasteful, let alone its implications. The fastest route to chaos. The ultimate in losing control.

'You don't have to deal with it yourself,' he told his solicitor. 'Turn it over to the police. Or Social Services. There are plenty of places for people like that.'

Irresponsible people who would think nothing of taking over a deserted house and living rent free.

'You might know this woman.'

Luke's huff of expelled breath was incredulous. 'I doubt that very much.'

'We've done some investigation. Her name's Amy Phillips. She works as a nurse in the cardiology ward of St Elizabeth's.'

Luke rubbed his temple with the middle finger of his free hand. The ache from his jaw was creeping upwards. He did not like this. Not that he'd heard of this nurse but this was a busy ward that dealt with patients from both the medical and surgical areas of cardiology. He couldn't possibly know the names of every junior staff member. It wasn't the fact that this Amy Phillips was employed here that was disturbing. It was the potential connection. A totally unexpected link from something he had no intention of touching in any form to… Luke raised his gaze again.

At first it was a suspicious scan of the area. Was that this Amy Phillips carrying the stepladder? Or the one with a pile of linen in her arms, heading towards the sluice room? The older woman, maybe, pushing a wheelchair who had just come into view at the end of the corridor. No. She had been here for years and years and her name definitely wasn't Amy. It was…something else.

The attempt to remember the name faded. All the noise and bustle became simply a muted background. The walls almost invisible. What Luke was aware of were in the beds behind the walls. Or in the playroom at the end of the corridor. Being carried by nurses who sang Christmas carols or held up to hook an angel to a high branch on a tree.

The *children*. Life was hard enough, wasn't it, without starting with the kinds of difficulties these sick children had to contend with. *They* were the reason he put so many unforgiving hours of his life into his work. It *was* his life, this place. His career. A stunningly successful one that changed the lives of many, many people.

Having it tainted by a shameful past was simply unthinkable.

'I don't give a damn who she is or where she works,' he said grimly. 'I want her gone and I want a demolition crew on site tomorrow. Deal with it.'

'It won't—'

'Yes, it will,' Luke contradicted. 'Money is not an object here. The proceeds from the sale of this property will be donated to an appropriate charity. Find an organisation who is prepared to take in these...*tenants* and I'll make sure they are a major beneficiary.'

'That might help,' Reginald Battersby conceded. He still sighed, however, as though the task was supremely distasteful. 'I'll see what I can do.'

The phone was still ringing.

Amy gave the large pot one more stir to make sure the meatballs weren't sticking at the bottom of the rich, tomato sauce they were simmering in.

'Hello?'

'Amy! It's me, Rosa.'

'Oh!' Amy made an excited face at two small boys who were lying on the flagged floor of this huge old kitchen. 'Angelo! Marco! It's your Mamma!'

Relaying the information so fast probably hadn't been wise. Now Amy had a six-year-old boy on either side, tugging at her arms, begging in voluble Italian for a turn on the phone. It made it a lot harder to hear what her older sister was saying.

'What was that? How's Nonna?'

'She hates being in the hospital.'

'How bad was it? The heart attack?'

'The procedure they did was successful, apparently. The arterio—plaster thing.'

'Angioplasty?'

'That's it! I knew *you* should have come with Mamma, not me. Neither of us have any real idea what they're talking about.'

'I couldn't go, you know that. Work's crazy and nobody's getting leave before Christmas. And there's trouble with the house. That horrible old lawyer was here again today. He's threatening to—'

The voices of her identical twin nephews became louder. '*Mamma*!' Angelo cried pitifully. '*Piacere, Zietta Amy—*'

'*No!*' Marco shoved his brother. '*Mi!*'

'Travelling with Mamma was a nightmare,' Rosa either hadn't heard or wasn't listening to Amy. 'She lost everything. Twice. Tickets, passport, luggage. I'm exhausted. And... I miss the boys.' She sounded close to tears. 'Are they okay?'

Her sister had enough to handle. A sick grandmother. A distraught mother. Being separated from her children so soon after being deserted by that no-good husband. It wouldn't be fair to share the fear that Amy wasn't going to be able to hold the fort here, even for a few days. That the walls of their world were crumbling at an alarmingly rapid rate.

'The boys are fine,' she said. 'Angels. Here, you talk to them for a minute. I need to check on Summer.'

Amy pushed the phone towards four small hands. 'Marco first,' she ordered. 'And don't hang up. I need to talk to Mamma again.' She spoke in Italian because it was their first language and more likely to be obeyed.

Another quick stir of the sauce made it spit and splatter onto the pitted surface of the ancient stove but Amy didn't have time to do more than wipe up one of the bigger spots with the corner of her apron. She crossed the room, taking just a moment to drop a kiss onto a bent golden head at the big, pine table.

'You're doing a fantastic job, Chantelle.' She spoke in English now, switching languages effortlessly. 'I really like your cutting out.'

'I need more colours.'

'I'll find some more old magazines. Did you find the glue?'

'Here. See?'

The jar of paste tipped and Amy hastily righted it. 'They'll be the best streamers any Christmas tree ever had. Weren't the others going to help you? Or are they doing their homework?'

'They're watching telly.'

'They'll have to get busy after dinner, then. Could you tell them it'll be ready soon?'

There was a somewhat battered old couch in the corner of this kitchen. It was covered with a mound of soft pillows at the end and lots of warm blankets, although the range did a wonderful job of heating this part of the old house. A small radiant heater was also on because the stone floor had an amazing ability to suck in heat.

An oxygen cylinder was tucked safely between the end of the couch and the wall. Tubing snaked towards nose prongs and the pale plastic accessory was made more obvious by how black the little face beneath it was.

Amy loved the feel of Summer's fuzzy hair. She stroked it again as she dropped to a crouch. 'How are you doing, sweetheart? Are you hungry?'

The small girl shook her head.

'Could you eat something? Some eggy soldiers, maybe?'

Another head shake but Summer was smiling her gorgeous smile. Enjoying the attention. Saving her limited breath for something worth saying.

'Soup? If I help you?'

The smile widened and Summer nodded.

'Chicken or tomato?'

'Chicken.' The word was a whisper. It was an effort to speak. An effort just to stay alive, really.

'Good girl.' Amy's fingers sought a pulse in the match-stick wrist as she kissed Summer's forehead. It was thready and too fast. As it always was. A quick glance at the regulator on the oxygen cylinder was a relief. The tank was still more than half-full and there was a new one in the bedroom upstairs. One less task to find time for. She gave her another kiss, this time concentrating on how the child's skin felt under her lips. Was it a little too warm? She took off one of the blankets.

'Zietta Amy!' Angelo called. 'Nonna wants to talk to you.'

Amy took the phone, greeted her mother and then listened to a garbled version of how her grandmother was doing, how tiresome the journey had been with so many people traveling to be home for Christmas and how worried she was about all 'her' children.

'We're fine,' Amy said when she could get a word in edgeways.

'What are you feeding my *bambinos*?'

'Tonight it's spaghetti and meatballs.'

'And vegetables?'

'Yes.' Tomatoes counted as vegetables, didn't they?

'How's Summer?' There was a new note in her mother's voice that went beyond the expected anxiety. Summer was their special one. Every day had to be treasured.

Amy cast a glance back at the couch. Summer lay quietly, just watching. As she had been all day.

'She's happy. She wants chicken soup for dinner.'

'Give her an egg. There's more goodness in an egg. It's

her favourite. Mash up the egg and cut the crusts off the bread and—'

'Chicken soup is good, too, Mamma. That's what she wants tonight.' Amy walked towards the pantry as she spoke, to get the can of soup while she thought of it. The pantry was vast. A relic from the days when this old house had had kitchen staff with scullery maids who would have used the old tubs in here to scour pans. Many of the shelves had nothing more than dust on them. Amy needed to find time to get to a supermarket. She had to get to work so she could pay for the groceries.

'She's too tired to eat? Is that it?'

Amy's hesitation said too much. Marcella Phillips clicked her tongue in distress. '*Dio*, but I hate being away from her.'

'I know, Mamma.'

'She's my little angel. How long is she being lent to us? This Christmas has to be the best. She's in my prayers every day but—'

'She's on the list for a heart transplant. *That* would be the best Christmas present.'

Amy put the can of soup on the bench and opened a drawer to search for a can opener. The bolognese sauce was bubbling enthusiastically. Bright spots of sauce were landing some considerable distance from the pot. The large pan of water beside it was finally coming to the boil. Amy dribbled some olive oil into the water, taking an anxious glance at her watch as she added a handful of salt.

'I need to go, Mamma. It's dinner time and I have to get ready for—' Amy bit her lip but it was too late.

'Ready for what, Amy Elisabetta? You're not going to *work* tonight?'

'I have to, Mamma.' There was no point alarming her mother by telling her how empty their household account was.

She would discuss it endlessly with Rosa and that would only make things worse. Rosa's husband had left her penniless and this was the only home she had for now. The boys needed their mother at home for a little longer, not out working because she felt compelled to help support the family.

'You said you would get time off until Rosa and I got back. It's only a few days. Maybe tomorrow, even.'

'Zoe is coming to stay with the children.'

'Zoe? *Zoe?* She's a child herself!' The fact that her mother had switched from English to Italian was a sure sign that stress levels were zooming up.

'She's sixteen, Mamma. Responsible.' It was quite difficult to hold the phone and open a can of soup at the same time.

'Pfff!' The sound was eloquent. 'Responsible people do not keep putting holes in themselves.'

'You get Zoe to babysit yourself. You love Zoe.'

'Not at night. Never *all* night.'

'Lizzie's is only five minutes' walk away. Three if I run. I've talked to my charge nurse. If there's an emergency at home, they'll let me come back.'

If they were quiet, that was.

'It won't do. We'll have to come home.'

'But what about Nonna?'

'She's going to be allowed out of hospital. Maybe even tomorrow. We're going to bring her home with us.'

Amy's heart sank. Nonna was the absolute stereotype of an old Italian woman from a small village. Tiny, wrinkled and always shrouded in voluminous black clothing, she spoke not a word of English. She would hate London.

'Are you sure about this, Mamma?' she asked carefully.

'Of course I'm sure.'

'But—'

'But what? You have a problem with your *nonna* coming to live with us?' Amy recognised that tone of admonition. It was dangerous. 'You don't *love* your Nonna?'

'Of course I do.'

'She can have Vanni's room.'

Amy was silent. This was just getting worse. Uncle Vanni's room might not be available for very much longer. Something had to be said. But what?

Again, Marcella interpreted the silence. 'You think we'll lose the house? No, no, no! That isn't going to happen, *cara*. I know Vanni made a will. It's in the house somewhere. We just have to find it.'

'We've looked everywhere. His desk, the bank, every single box in the attic...'

'He was disorganised, my cousin. It will be somewhere we don't expect.'

The water was boiling now. Ready for the pasta. Chantelle was climbing down from her chair at the table, trailing a string of coloured paper loops for admiration. Angelo and Marco had vanished and happy shrieks were coming from the lounge where the television was.

'I *have* to go, Mamma,' Amy said firmly. 'Give Nonna a kiss for me. Call me tomorrow.'

'You keep looking. Try the dresser.'

'What dresser?'

'The one in the kitchen. With the recipe books and the old... What are they?' It was a sure sign of overwhelming stress when words failed Marcella. 'The letters to say the bills are paid?'

'Receipts.'

'*Sì*. There's a lot of receipts in there. Other papers, too, maybe.'

* * *

It was getting late by the time Luke Harrington had finished his ward round. Very late.

'What are you still doing here, Luke?'

'I could ask you the same thing, Margaret.'

The charge nurse laughed. 'I'm legit. I'm doing a long day so I don't finish till 9:00 p.m., after handover for the night shift. What's your excuse?'

'Johnny Smythe got admitted. Heart failure.'

'I heard that. He's having a bad run, isn't he? Even for a Down's syndrome child, he's getting more than his fair share.'

'They can't put off the surgery any longer. I'll have to try and fit him in in the next couple of days. Tomorrow, possibly.'

'Isn't wee Liam going to Theatre tomorrow?'

Luke slotted the case notes he'd been writing in back into the trolley. 'It's certainly shaping up to be a long day.' Another one. He rubbed the back of his neck, wondering why he felt more drained than usual. Ah…yes…

'Do you know a nurse called Amy Phillips?' he asked Margaret.

'Of course.' Margaret gave him a puzzled glance. 'Why do you ask?'

'Someone mentioned her name today, that's all. I couldn't place it.'

Margaret shook her head. 'Honestly, Luke. Sometimes I think you operate on a different planet. She was a theatre nurse for ages before she came onto the ward here.' Her look was resigned. 'It's no wonder you're still single if you don't even notice women as gorgeous as our Amy.'

Luke didn't discuss his personal life. So far, the hospital grapevine had been denied any juicy titbits regarding his background.

'Someone else clearly thought the same way,' he said dismissively. 'It sounded to me as though she has more children than she can manage.'

Margaret laughed. 'She has, at that. Her mother has, at any rate. She's a foster-parent. They're lucky children that end up in the Phillipses' house.'

Luke frowned. The squatters were fostering children? It didn't make sense. It was also disturbing. He had ordered the demolition of a house full of disadvantaged children?

'The latest addition was Summer Bell. Do you remember her? That dear little Somalian girl who was here a few months ago?' She gave Luke a wry smile. 'You're better at remembering patient names than staff members.'

'I operated on her twice. Of course I remember.' Luke was feeling faintly dizzy. He needed to sit down. Or escape. And it was high time he had something to eat. 'She's terminal,' he said quietly. 'Unless a transplant becomes available in time, and we both know how unlikely that is. She was…sadly… sent home to die.' A case that was not one of the success stories. Never a good idea to dwell on those.

'She had no home to go to,' Margaret said softly. 'Her foster-family couldn't face looking after a terminally ill child. Amy had fallen in love with her. So did Marcella.'

'Marcella?' The Italian name sent a chill down Luke's spine.

'Amy's mother.'

'She's…' Luke swallowed. 'She's Italian?'

'Marcella is. Amy is half-Italian. Marcella married an English policeman, of all things. He brought his family to London when Amy was about five.' Margaret was smiling. 'You wouldn't know she was half-English to look at her, mind you. She's dark and gorgeous and more than a bit fiery.'

Passionate.

It felt as if the walls were closing in. 'I have to go,' Luke decided aloud. His sudden movement clearly startled Margaret enough to need an explanation. 'Early start tomorrow.'

He needed some time alone. To say he was shaken would be an accurate description, except that Luke Harrington did not *get* shaken. The physical movement of striding through the familiar corridors of St Elizabeth's should have been enough to centre himself, but it wasn't.

Something had changed.

Tentacles were pulling at him. Threads of a connection he hadn't expected and most definitely didn't want. More than one of them, too. It felt like some kind of portal had opened and it was following him.

All thanks to an inheritance he wanted nothing to do with. A house he'd probably driven past a thousand times until he'd learned the significance of the address and had gone out of his way *not* to pass it on his way to and from the apartment.

He slid into the driver's seat of his sleek car and drove smoothly to the car-park exit. He had a lot to do tonight. He wanted to plan the major surgery on tiny Liam. He needed to think about the best way to tackle Johnny's oversized septal defect, as well.

He was *not* going to allow himself to be distracted. To feel guilty that he might be scattering a foster-family right before Christmas. They would be better off somewhere else. They were living in a substandard house, for heaven's sake. Practically derelict according to the independent surveyor's report on the dwelling he had received via Mr Battersby.

Missing slates on the roof, a chimney that had a dangerous lean, broken windows that hadn't been repaired properly. He could probably see how inappropriate it was from the outside if he took the time to drive past now that he knew the precise address he was looking for.

No. He didn't want to do that. He didn't want to go near the place.

Not in this lifetime.

There *were* a lot of papers in that hutch dresser. Amy was sitting in a sea of them. She'd only meant to have a quick look but somehow the table hadn't been cleared, the children were not in bed as they should have been and she was running out of time to shower and change into her uniform.

And now someone was pounding on her door.

It couldn't be Zoe, who knew to come in the back. In fact, why wasn't Zoe here yet?

'There's someone at the door, Amy.'

'I know, Chantelle. Oh, you're in your pyjamas. Good girl.'

'Shall I see who it is?'

'No.' It was dark and there shouldn't be anyone knocking at this time of the evening. Amy's heart rate picked up as she went into the shadowy space of the wide hallway. She had a nasty feeling it was going to be that elderly solicitor who'd been here earlier. Or worse. Maybe it was the police coming to evict them.

Standing on tiptoe, Amy peered through the spy hole. She rubbed at the tiny piece of glass, not believing what she was seeing. She peered harder. And then she opened the door, without putting the safety chain on first.

She knew she was probably gaping like a stranded fish but this was so weird!

'Mr *Harrington*,' she gasped. 'What are you doing here?'

CHAPTER TWO

HE WAS still angry with her!

Gorgeous looking, unapproachable, important men did not turn up on Amy's doorstep. Luke Harrington was so far out of her league that this was as disconcerting as it would have been to find a member of the royal family knocking on her door.

However unprofessional and unprecedented it might be, the only explanation Amy could come up with was that Mr Harrington had found out where she lived and had come to yell at her. On top of the worry about her family and yet another fruitless search for a document that represented safety for all of them, this was too much.

Amy almost burst into tears.

Like she had last week, when she had utterly failed to come up to the standards this surgeon expected from his staff.

Had he come to tell her not to bother showing up for work tonight? That he'd persuaded the principal nursing officer that Amy needed to be let go without even serving any notice?

It could be the final straw. Her family might soon have no income, as well as nowhere to live.

But why wasn't he saying anything?

He was staring at her. As though she had just walked into

his operating theatre stark naked or something. As though he couldn't believe what he was seeing and it was so far from being acceptable he couldn't decide what to do about it.

He hadn't expected her to be terrified of him!

Luke recognised her, of course. Sort of. Not that he'd ever seen her out of a uniform that usually included a surgical mask and hat, but those eyes were unique. Dark pools of the variety Luke instinctively avoided ever letting his gaze do more than rake past.

The kind of pools men with lesser control had difficulty not falling into.

He couldn't drag his gaze away this time, however. Because of the fear he could see there. Real fear. The kind he often saw in the eyes of children when they were facing a necessary but painful procedure.

The kind of expression that made you want to protect them. To comfort them and tell them everything was going to be all right. And what good would that do? Someone had to do the hard yards. To distance themselves enough to be able to do what had to be done to actually *make* everything all right.

Precisely what he'd come here to do. He had gone against his better judgement, having parked across the road just to confirm the opinion of that surveyor's report, by deciding to front up in person. To tell this Amy Phillips that this situation was not the end of the world. That he'd make sure that she— and the children—would find new accommodation in time for Christmas.

Better accommodation, dammit!

Luke drew in a deep breath. She'd asked him, quite reasonably, what he was doing there. With an effort, he dragged his gaze away from her eyes. Away from the tumble of dark hair with enough curl in it to make it shine from the dim light of the hallway behind her.

Like a halo.

Away from the way her soft woollen jumper and tight jeans clung to curves that a scrub suit or nurses' uniform had never revealed. Away from an apron that was smeared with red stains and had what looked like… Good grief, tomato skins glued to it? It was filthy!

Luke let his breath out with a rush that gave his words more force than he might have intended. The words themselves were not what he'd planned to say, either, but a wave of something like outrage was building. Were these disadvantaged children in a not simply substandard but *dirty* house?

'I'm here because this is *my* house,' he said.

She certainly hadn't been expecting that. He could see shock and then bewilderment on her face. The unconscious, small head shake that made the tumble of waves shiver and gleam.

And then her jaw dropped and her eyes—as impossible as that seemed—managed to get even larger. Darker. Lakes instead of pools now.

'Oh, my God!' she whispered. *'Harrington.'*

He waited. Curious to know what connection she was making. Maybe she hadn't expected this, but she was figuring out why it was happening.

'Harrington village…that was where Uncle Vanni's wife grew up.'

Uncle Vanni? Was this woman some kind of blood relative? A cousin? Or, worse, a half-sister, perhaps? The notion was distasteful.

Unacceptable.

'The owner of this house was your *uncle*?'

Another tiny head shake. 'Not really. He's…he was my mother's cousin. Or second cousin. A distant relative, really, but they grew up in the same village in Italy.'

She made a soft sound of inexpressible sadness. 'Everybody called him Uncle. He… You…'

Lakes were becoming pools again and Luke found himself transfixed, watching Amy Phillips focus.

'There was a story that Caroline came from an enormously wealthy family. They lived in some vast manor house. We never knew her surname but villages used to get named after the manor houses, didn't they? Harrington village. Harrington Manor.' Amy's chest rose as she took a steadying breath. 'You're a Harrington,' she said quietly. 'It's your family?'

Still, Luke remained silent, letting her join the dots herself. She ran her tongue over her lips as though they had become suddenly dry. It might be rude to stare, but Luke couldn't look away for the life of him.

'Of course it is,' Amy continued. 'You're a Harrington. We were told that the property would probably go to one of Uncle Vanni's wife's relatives if a more recent will couldn't be found.'

'It did.' Luke finally spoke. 'It came to me.'

'So you're a nephew or something?'

'I'm Giovanni Moretti's son.'

'No.' Amy released her breath in what sounded almost like a sigh of relief. 'There's been a mistake. Uncle Vanni's son is dead. He was killed in a terrible car accident. The same accident that killed his mother.'

'Amy?' A small voice was calling from inside the house. 'Can I hang my streamers on the tree?'

'Soon, hon. Put your dressing-gown and slippers on,

though. It's freezing in there. I haven't had time to light that fire.'

It *was* freezing. Why hadn't Luke noticed the goose-bumps on Amy's forearms where the sleeves of the jumper had been pushed up? Or the way she was wrapping her arms around herself now? And she was shivering.

It was all very well for him. Luke had his full-length, black cashmere coat over his suit, a warm scarf around his neck and soft, fur-lined leather gloves on his hands.

Not only was this Amy Phillips cold, she was letting icy air into a house that had children living in it.

'May I come in?' The request was reluctant but he didn't have to go any further than the front entranceway, did he? 'I would like to talk to you.'

But Amy was clearly more reluctant than he was. She actually had the nerve to start shutting the door on him.

'There's nothing to talk about,' she said. 'There *is* another will and we'll find it. Soon. You can't turn Uncle Vanni's children out into the streets. I won't let you.'

Luke caught the door just before it closed. He put his foot in the gap as insurance. He wasn't going to leave until he'd sorted this out. Imagine what people would think if this was the story that reached the hospital grapevine—that a paediatric surgeon had arrived in person to try and turn children out to live in cardboard boxes under a bridge somewhere.

To freeze to death in the coldest December anyone could remember. Too cold even to snow, which was disappointing everyone who was hoping for a white Christmas this year.

'What was his name?' he demanded.

'Uncle Vanni's son? His name was Luca.'

The word was said with an Italian pronunciation. It echoed. Touching some long-buried memory.

Luca...

How old had he been? Three? Old enough to remember his mother's voice?

Luca...

Amy was staring again. Realising the implication. Luke was simply the anglicised version of the name. He was telling the truth, but she wasn't about to accept it because it wasn't something she wanted to hear. Would showing her that long-faded scar that ran from his left temple to his hairline make any difference? Ironic that he should find himself in the position of *wanting* to prove he was Giovanni's son.

'Zietta Amy! Vieni! Rapidimente!'

The language made Luke flinch but, as always, it was more intelligible that he was comfortable with. Mind you, that kind of verbal alarm would transcend any language barriers.

'Che cosa succede?' Amy turned in alarm. *'Vengo!'*

She was going to see why she was being summoned so urgently. Luke found himself standing alone on the doorstep as Amy ran after a small boy with curly, dark hair. Down the hallway and through a door that seemed to have a wisp of smoke coming through it.

And then he could smell it. Something was burning! A fire had started in a house full of children.

With a strangled oath, Luke stepped inside and pushed the door closed behind him.

Amy stomped on the flaming remains of the paper streamer that had been inadvertently draped over the small heater, slipping through the grille to touch the bars.

'I was just showing it to Summer,' Chantelle wailed. 'I'm sorry, Amy.'

'It was a stupid streamer, anyway.' Fourteen-year-old

Robert was reacting to his fright by retreating into teenage surliness. 'Girls are *so* dumb!'

'I'm not dumb,' Chantelle sobbed, 'Am I, Amy?'

'No.' But Amy was more worried about the smoky air and how it could affect Summer's breathing. It was hard enough for her poor, malformed heart to get oxygen into her blood without having smoke added to the mix. Amy reached for the regulator on the cylinder.

'I'm going to turn up the flow for a bit, darling,' she told Summer. 'It might tickle your nose.'

Summer nodded. The alarm in her face had begun to fade as soon as Amy was in the room and she was now watching with interest as Marco stirred scraps of charred paper with his foot to draw shapes on the flagstones.

'Don't do that,' Amy chided. 'It's enough of a mess in here as it is. Could one of you please find the dustpan and brush in the scullery and we'll clean it up.' She looked up from adjusting the regulator to see how many of the children were in the kitchen and who would be first to respond to the request.

And then she froze.

Luke Harrington was standing in the doorway. Staring again. Silently. Looking absolutely…appalled.

And no wonder! It was all too easy to follow his line of vision and see things from his perspective. Amy could feel a hot flush of mortification bloom. If he hadn't already considered her to be incompetent after that disaster in the ward the other day, she was offering ample proof right now.

The kitchen was in utter chaos.

Robert and Andrew had still not begun their allocated task of dishwashing. Pots and plates smeared with tomato sauce and festooned with strings of spaghetti littered the bench. Bowls with spoons and puddles of melted ice cream had been pushed to one end of the table. The other end was crowded with ripped-up magazines, scissors, rolls of sticky tape and a pot of glue that had spilt, making a larger puddle that was now congealing around shreds of discarded paper.

The doors of the hutch dresser were open and it had been Amy who had created the piles of recipe books, ancient domestic paperwork, long out-of-date telephone directories and any number of other random finds including a set of ruined paintbrushes and several half-empty tins of varnish.

The room was hot and steamy and it smelt of cooking and smoke. It was dingy because one of the bare light bulbs that hung from the high ceiling was burnt out and Amy hadn't had a chance to haul in the ladder so she could replace it. The walls were covered with examples of children's artwork but most of the pictures hung at drunken angles because the tape was rendered useless when it became damp.

And there were children everywhere in various stages of undress. Chantelle had pyjamas on but, instead of a dressing-gown, she had pulled on a vast woollen jersey that had been a favourite of Uncle Vanni's. It hung down to her knees and her hands were hidden somewhere within the sleeves.

Twelve-year-old Kyra had a woollen beanie on her head, ug boots on her feet and a flannelette nightgown between the accessories. Standing together, the girls were the picture of children who looked like they had no one who cared about them.

The twins seemed oblivious to their visitor and marched about importantly. Marco had the dustpan and Angelo the hearthbrush, but they couldn't decide how to co-ordinate their efforts and were finding the task highly amusing.

Eleven-year-old Andrew was beside Robert. He elbowed the older boy, who obligingly scowled at Luke.

'Who are you?' he demanded, flushing as his voice cracked. 'And what are you doing here?'

Amy caught her breath. This was actually rather stunning. Robert had been passed from foster-home to foster-home in his short life, becoming progressively more 'difficult' and setting up a vicious cycle where the things that children needed most—an accepting, secure, *loving* environment that had boundaries—were getting further and further from his reach.

He'd come to the Phillips household six months ago, which was already a record for him, taken in as Marcella's way of coping with her grief at losing her beloved cousin and a signal that she intended to carry on what had become a passion for Vanni. Caring for 'lost' children. Being told that 'a man of the house' was needed had been startling for the teenaged Robert.

Right now—standing up to this stranger in their kitchen— it was possible he was reaching out to accept that position of responsibility. That he felt safe enough himself to feel the need to protect his 'family'.

Amy still hadn't let out her breath. Imagine if he learned why Luke was really here? That he had inherited this house and was planning to kick them all out? That the children might be separated and Robert could find himself back in a home where no one was prepared to accept him, let alone make him the man of the house.

She couldn't let it happen.

Catching Luke's gaze, Amy knew she was sending out a desperate plea.

'This is Mr Harrington,' she told Robert. 'He's Summer's doctor and he's just come to make sure she's all right.'

'Oh...' Robert straightened his shoulders and became visibly taller. 'That's OK, then.'

Amy could see Luke assessing the situation. Deciding whether or not to go along with her white lie.

Please, she begged silently. *Don't hurt these children. At least give me time to prepare them. To reassure them and find a solution.*

Luke's face was expressionless. He looked at Robert for what seemed like a long time and then turned slowly to meet Amy's gaze again, and she'd never been so acutely aware of this man's looks before.

Oh, he was gorgeous. Everybody knew that. Very tall, very dark. His features as carefully sculpted as the way he carried himself. A bit over the top, really—like that designer coat, probably French, that he was wearing so casually unbuttoned to reveal a pinstriped suit. There was a distinct aura of perfection about Luke Harrington. The way he looked. The way he worked. The standards he expected from everyone around him. Perfection. Control.

What on earth was she thinking, even hoping that he might back up something that was rather a lot less than the truth?

No wonder there was no hint of a smile on his face when he opened his mouth to respond. Amy's heart skipped a beat as it sank, waiting for the blow to fall.

'That's right,' Luke said gravely. He began to walk over the flagstones. Slowly. As though he was sleepwalking. His gaze still touching Amy's. 'How *is* Summer today?'

Tears of gratitude stung Amy's eyes and she hurriedly blinked them away. As Luke reached the couch and bent down, his face loomed closer and Amy could see what had not been apparent at a distance. He knew exactly what he was doing by not contradicting her.

He *understood*.

And it was enough for hope to be born.

Enough to make Amy's heart sing and her lips to curve into a smile that said exactly how important this was. He understood, so surely he would not be able to go ahead and hurt this family.

She was smiling at him.

As though he'd just given her the greatest gift anyone could ever receive.

It made her eyes sparkle and the warmth emanating from that smile seemed to enter every cell of Luke's body.

He felt…weird.

Powerful and generous and…and like he'd done something wonderful.

How ridiculous was that?

All he'd done had been to keep the real nature of this visit private from a bunch of children who should not be involved in business between adults.

It didn't mean that he was about to change his mind. No matter how gorgeous that smile was. Luke dragged his gaze away from Amy's face.

'Hey, Summer. It's been a while since I saw you.'

Automatically, he took the tiny wrist between his fingers to feel her pulse and watched the small chest to assess how much effort was going into breathing. Post-surgery, patients like Summer Bell returned to the care of a cardiologist so unless Luke made an effort, it was hard to keep up with how well they were doing.

And this little girl was not doing very well. Little Summer was the kind of case that could break your heart if you let it. Some months ago, Luke had done his best to make final corrections to the major congenital anomalies of her heart and the vessels that connected it to her lungs, but there was only so much that could be done. And in this case, it hadn't been enough.

If she stayed alive long enough, she would be a candidate for a heart transplant, but her condition was clearly deteriorating.

'Have you got a pulse oximeter?' Luke queried.

'No.'

'A stethoscope?'

Again, Amy shook her head and Luke tried to push aside his frustration. This was a house, not a hospital ward, after all. Summer was probably fortunate to have a qualified nurse caring for her.

Or she would be, if that qualified nurse wasn't running some kind of orphanage. Luke looked over his shoulder. The two small boys behind him were scuffling over their sweeping duties. Giggling. They were indistinguishable and, Luke had to admit, very cute. Curly and dark and energetic. Rather like the woman they had called, what had it been—*Zietta*? Aunty? He shifted his gaze to Amy who was watching him assess Summer, her eyes wide and anxious.

'How many children do you have living here?'

Amy blinked. She looked nervous, Luke decided. Was she thinking he was about to criticise her ability to care for a sick child because there were too many other demands on her attention?

He could see no reason to do so, so far. Summer was warm and comfortable and looked happy. She was receiving oxygen. Presumably being given all her medications or she would be a lot worse than she was. What more could anyone be doing?

'Right now?' Amy was responding. 'Seven.'

'And you're trying to care for them all? By yourself?'

Her chin lifted a fraction. She had taken his incredulous question as criticism rather than concern.

'Of course not,' she said. 'My mother is the official foster-parent. My sister also lives here. Marco and Angelo are her children. My nephews.'

'So where is your mother? And your sister?' He would have to speak to them all. Three Italian women who were not going to like what he had to say, God help him!

'Um…' Amy's gaze slid sideways. 'They're in Italy just at the moment.'

'*Bisnonna*'s sick,' Angelo piped up helpfully. 'She is a sick…' He looked at Amy questioningly. '*Cuore?*'

'Heart,' Amy supplied. 'She *has* a sick heart. It's my grand-mother,' she explained to Luke. 'She's had an MI. My mother had to go to her and she needed my sister to travel with her. I couldn't leave because I have to work.'

Luke's eyebrows rose involuntarily.

'It's only for a day or so. They're going to bring Nonna back.'

Luke sucked in a breath. 'Here?'

'Yes,' Amy said firmly. 'Here. We're going to give her Uncle Vanni's room.'

Luke let his breath out slowly. So he was not only going to have to find suitable accommodation for a collection of children, including one who was terminally ill, he now had to throw an elderly, recuperating cardiac patient into the mix.

With a bemused shake of his head, he turned back to something much easier to deal with. Summer.

'Can I listen to you heart, chicken?' he asked. 'With my ear?'

Amy looked startled but Summer didn't seem to mind the unusual request and the twins were fascinated to see Luke bend his head to place his ear directly on Summer's bare, frail chest.

'What you doing?' Marco asked.

'I'm listening to Summer's heart. And her lungs.'

'Can I listen, too?'

'No.' It was Amy who spoke. 'I want you boys to go and get into the bath before it gets cold. Go now. Shoo!' she added as the twins shuffled reluctantly. 'I'll be up in a minute to make sure you've washed behind your ears.'

'Can we make it hot again?'

'Just a little bit. The big boys still haven't had their bath.'

The information that the hot-water supply in the house was less than ideal barely filtered into the back of Luke's mind thanks to his concentration. Even without the magnification a stethoscope would have provided, he could hear all he needed to reassure himself there was nothing major happening on top of the expected murmurs of abnormal blood flow through Summer's heart.

He lifted the blankets a moment later to check her ankles. There was no swelling to suggest that her heart failure was not under control but he still wasn't entirely happy and he knew he was frowning as he looked at Amy.

Her face was so…alive. She could talk without saying a word. Luke could see she understood his disquiet perfectly. That she also sensed something was brewing but, as yet, there was nothing to point out the direction any deterioration was taking. It was impressive that this nurse could share what was an instinctive warning bell. It was somewhat disturbing that they could communicate almost telepathically.

Amy probably found it equally disturbing. 'We're looking after her,' she said aloud. 'We all love Summer.' She stooped to kiss the child. 'I'm going get your medicine now, darling, and put you to bed. Zoe's coming to look after you and read you a story.'

'Zoe?'

'The babysitter. I'm on night shift tonight.'

Luke was shocked. 'You're going to work? Tonight?'

Her look was steady and Luke almost felt embarrassed. Yes, she could communicate very well non-verbally. Bills needed to be paid, the look said. Mouths needed to be fed. Not everybody had the luxury of being able to afford designer coats. Some people had no choice about having to work, no matter how difficult it might be.

'Robert's here, as well.' Amy motioned towards the lanky boy who was now washing dishes. 'He's fourteen and he's our man of the house.'

Luke could hear the pride in Amy's tone. He could see the way the corner of Robert's mouth twitched—as though he was suppressing a pleased smile. The teenager didn't turn towards them, however. Instead, he spoke gruffly to the younger boy beside him.

'Get those bowls off the table,' he ordered. 'They need doing, as well.'

'That's Andrew,' Amy told Luke. 'He's eleven.' She smiled at the boy. 'You're doing a great job, Andy. Thank you.'

The twins had disappeared, presumably into the bath, but the two girls were still at the table and Luke raised an eyebrow. Seeing as they had started introductions, they might as well finish.

'Chantelle's eight and Kyra's twelve,' Amy said co-operatively. 'They've both been living with us for nearly two years now.'

'Amy?' Chantelle had her hands full of paper loops. 'Can we put these on the tree now?'

Amy nodded. 'And then it's bed for you and homework for Kyra. I'm going to put Summer to bed now and get changed for work.'

'OK.' The girls headed through the door.

Luke suddenly felt as though he didn't belong there. He should get out of the way and let Amy sort out her unconventional household.

'I still need to talk to you,' he warned.

Surprisingly, Amy nodded. 'Give me a few minutes to get Summer to bed and the other children organised. Unless it can wait until tomorrow?'

'I don't think so.' Luke wanted to get it over with. He had no intention of coming back here tomorrow. Or any other day, for that matter.

Amy disconnected the tubing from the oxygen cylinder and gathered Summer into her arms. A few minutes later, the boys finished their task of clearing the bench and also left the kitchen. Luke found himself alone, the noise of activity and voices fading into the distance.

He scanned the room. The old range still had spots of burnt sauce all over it. The table was a mess and it looked as though somebody had had a tantrum with the contents of the hutch dresser. Why was it being emptied all over the floor like that? Had Amy been searching for something?

Like a will?

Was there another will that would have left the house to its current occupants? His information was that the only will ever recorded by Giovanni Moretti had been made shortly after his marriage to Caroline Harrington in which he had left all his worldly goods to his wife and any children they might be blessed with. His wife had died over thirty years ago, however, and he'd never bothered to locate his child.

It was quite possible he would be less than happy with what had eventuated.

Well, tough! If he wasn't getting what he wanted, it was exactly what he deserved. Even if he *had* made another will, Luke could contest it and no doubt win the case easily as the closest living relative.

Still...Luke felt uncomfortable. Movement seemed a good distraction and it could be useful. Already he could see things that made this house substandard, like the old cooker, the dripping taps, the bare light bulbs and the peeling paint on the ceiling. Was the rest of the house in even worse condition? A list of such inadequacies would strengthen his case that better accommodation would be more suitable for these people.

And with that in mind, Luke dismissed his aversion to being inside this house and set off to explore.

CHAPTER THREE

IT WAS worse than he had expected.

Or perhaps better, given that he was looking for ammunition with which to strengthen his position.

A large room next to the kitchen and scullery complex had a television in one corner. A fire burned merrily, safely covered by a wire screen, but the warmth and cleanliness of the room was easy to overlook.

Luke's attention was on several very old and mismatched couches that could well have been rescued from a rubbish dump, with their lumpy cushions and frayed fabrics. Battered toys lay scattered about, some of the lead-light windows had cracks covered with masking tape and, if he concentrated, he could feel a draft of icy air around his ankles.

The two older boys lay on the floor in front of the television with what looked like schoolwork around them. Robert noticed Luke entering the room and he could feel the challenging glare on his back as he walked over to a set of French doors. This was where the draft was coming from but Luke could see why the curtains had not been drawn. The ancient velvet would probably disintegrate under the pressure required to pull them into place.

Enough light escaped the room to illuminate a flagged terrace area and the shaggy edges of a large, dark garden. Luke knew it was a large garden because a plan of the property had been included with the paperwork his solicitor had sent him weeks ago now.

Large was not really the word for it, he thought, staring out at the smudged outlines of old trees. It was vast by London standards. With the house removed, it would be easy to build an entire apartment block on the site. With Regent's Park virtually across the road, it wasn't reasonable for anyone to sit on private parkland that supported only one dwelling. Financially, it was just plain stupid.

The observation he was still under from Robert made Luke vaguely uncomfortable but he was satisfied with the list of inadequacies he had noted in this room, so he acknowledged the boys with a nod and somewhat tight smile, leaving the room to cross the wide hallway where he entered what must have originally been a drawing room.

There were more leaded windows here and the fanlights had coloured glass in an intricate pattern. The ceiling in this room was very high and the plasterwork very ornate, but it failed to impress Luke. How could it when it was a pale imitation of the architectural splendour Harrington Manor had to offer and when its condition was so bad? The paint on this ceiling was peeling off in large flakes. Probably lead-based paint, Luke decided. Dangerous for children.

Such as the two girls who were sitting on a faded rug in front of a cavernous fireplace that contained some half-burnt logs and no doubt provided a whistling, icy draft. The girls didn't notice Luke enter the room because they were too intent on admiring their handiwork.

A tall but scraggly tree branch—possibly yew—was propped up in a plastic bucket that had a tartan ribbon tied around it. More of the tartan ribbon was tied in bows on the branch offshoots and it was now also draped with the strings of paper loops he'd seen Chantelle carrying.

'We need an angel,' he heard her say to Kyra. 'For the top.'

'Angels are expensive,' Kyra said doubtfully. 'There might not be enough money if we're all going to get a present.'

'We could make one.'

Kyra shook her head. 'That would be a really hard thing to make. We could make a star, though. A really big one and I think we've got some glitter.'

'Silver glitter?' Chantelle asked hopefully.

'No. I think it's blue. Or green. It's left over from that birthday card we made Robert.'

'Oh… That was blue. 'Cos he's a boy, remember?'

'Oh, yeah… That's right.'

Blue didn't seem to be acceptable. Luke watched as Chantelle wriggled closer to Kyra and the older girl put her arm around her shoulders.

'It's still beautiful,' Kyra said. 'And we're lucky. Some kids don't even get a tree.'

And some had so many beautiful new decorations, they had no use for a big box of older ones. Imagine how excited these girls would be if they had that whole box that had been left in the ward office. It wouldn't be hard to pick it up and leave it on the doorstep here.

The apparent brilliance of the idea was surprising. The strength of desire to follow it through was unsettling. What was he thinking? The cleaners had most likely taken the box away as rubbish by now and even if they hadn't, all he'd achieve would be to give the impression that he wanted these children to stay here and enjoy Christmas. He could make sure they got a much better tree somewhere else. In their new home. A real spruce tree that had gifts beneath it and an angel on the top.

The girls needed to be cuddled together for more than comfort. That fire would have to be well stoked for a long time to take the chill off this enormous room. He took note of a slightly damp smell, as well, as he slipped out.

A peal of childish laughter drifted down the sweep of the staircase at the end of the hallway, but fortunately Luke could think of no reason he needed to go upstairs. Except that he felt curiously disappointed. Although he had seen enough to fuel the argument he knew was looming, he decided to check out the last downstairs room. Perhaps the distinct feeling of discomfort at what he was doing here would be relieved if he found something more personal to the previous owner of this house.

Something that might rekindle the anger that had grown from the loneliness of being so different. Alone. Brought up isolated from parents or siblings. Unwanted to the extent that not even a spark of responsibility remained.

He hit the jackpot through the door that opened beneath the staircase. Having turned on the light and instantly sensing that this room's occupant had been absent for some time, Luke froze.

This was it. Away from an upstairs inhabited by numerous women and children, this had been a man's domain. The old brass bed had a maroon cover. A dark woollen dressing-gown hung on one of the brass knobs and a pair of well-used men's slippers lay beneath it. A maroon colour, like the bedspread, the woollen toes of the slippers were a little frayed and the sheepskin lining squashed into an off-white felt. They could have been anyone's slippers.

Except they weren't.

These slippers had been worn by Giovanni Moretti.

His father.

Luke's mouth was dry. He hadn't expected anything like this. He'd grown up knowing that his father was a monster. Responsible for his mother's death and too uncaring to think of his son. He had been an ogre until Luke had been old enough to start feeling angry. To start hating the man. Even then, he had always seemed larger than life. An enemy. A man powerful enough to ruin the lives of others.

But huge, powerful, evil men did not wear slippers like this.

They didn't collect homeless children and get called 'Uncle' by everyone, either. His father had owned this house and presumably lived in London since *he* had been five years old, and he'd never made contact. Never remembered a birthday or sent a letter. And yet he'd left him this house.

Why?

To underline the fact that he had existed—close by—and hadn't given a damn? To make sure Luke never forgot?

As if he could!

Luke could actually taste the bitterness that rose within him. Giovanni Moretti had cared about the children other people didn't want, but he hadn't cared about his own son.

He was right to hate this man. To dismiss his life—and this room—with no more than a cursory look.

A gaze that took in a plain dressing-table that had a brush and comb on its dusty surface and unframed photographs jammed into the frame around the large mirror. Snapshots of people. Dozens of them. Luke found his feet moving in much the same way as he'd been drawn towards Amy and Summer in the kitchen. Pulled by something he couldn't—or didn't want to—identify.

One photograph stood out from the rest. In pride of place maybe, at the top left-hand corner. Or maybe it looked different because it was older. Curled at the edges. The hairs on the back of Luke's neck prickled as he stepped closer, however. What, in God's name, was a photograph of himself doing in this man's room?

It wasn't him. Of course it wasn't. The explanation was genetic. This was a picture of his father taken more than thirty years ago when he had looked extraordinarily like Luke did now.

The gorgeous blonde woman in the photograph was just as easily recognisable. Caroline Harrington had been frozen in time and had always looked like this as far as Luke had known. Except there was a difference here. Compared to the studio portraits Grandmother had in plenty, this was just a candid shot. The focus wasn't perfect and the colours had faded. What was even more different was his mother's expression.

Sheer joy radiated from her face as she looked up at the man beside her.

Even the baby in her arms seemed to be laughing. Tiny fists punched the air in an exuberance of happiness. Luke had never seen a photograph of himself as a baby. For a long, long moment, he simply stood there. Staring.

Shocked.

Faintly, the sound of feet running down the stairs and Amy's voice filtered through the haze.

'I'll be back up in a minute,' Amy was calling. 'I just need to talk to Mr Harrington before he goes home.'

There was no time to try and analyse any of the odd, unsettling emotions Luke was experiencing. And there was no point, was there? It was all in the past and best forgotten. Destroying the evidence would make it all so much simpler.

Without really thinking about what he was doing, Luke tugged the photograph free of the mirror and slipped it into his coat pocket. He flicked the light off as he left the room and strode back towards the kitchen. The sooner he left this house the better.

All he had to do was make sure Amy understood that the same applied to her.

Amy wound a rubber band around the end of the sleek French plait taming her hair that she had accomplished before hauling the twins from the bath and getting them dry and into their pyjamas. She changed into the tunic top and trousers of her uniform as the boys scrambled into the bunk beds in the room they shared with Robert and Andrew. She laced comfortable shoes onto her feet as she sat on the end of the trundle bed in her room where Summer was now tucked up.

The bedroom oxygen cylinder was full and the coal fire stoked and screened. Summer was warm and already asleep. Amy kissed her, hating it that she had to leave to go to work.

'Zoe will be here any minute,' she whispered, more to re-assure herself than anyone else. 'She's going to sleep in my bed so she'll be right here beside you.'

She kissed her again, and stroked her hair softly. One of these nights, Summer was going to go to sleep and simply not wake up.

Not tonight. Please… Not before Christmas!

Giving her uniform a final tug into place and letting the twins know she'd be back up to say good-night, Amy ran down the stairs. It was amazing how being clean and tidy and ready for work made her feel so much more in control.

Ready for anything.

Or almost anything. The empty kitchen took the wind out

of her sails momentarily. So did the odd expression on Mr Harrington's face when he appeared a few seconds later. Had he been snooping? Would that explain the curiously guilty flash she thought she saw in his eyes?

'This house is appalling,' Luke said without preamble, walking towards Amy. 'It's falling to pieces.' He stopped when he reached the kitchen table, resting a hand on the back of one of the chairs. 'It's neither a safe nor a healthy environment for anyone to live in. Particularly children. *Especially* a sick child. It's simply not fit for human habitation.'

'*We* love it.' Amy's heart sank at the wobble in her voice. She could do with a chair to hang onto herself. How had that confidence she'd brought downstairs with her evaporated so instantly?

Maybe there was a disadvantage to wearing her uniform, as well. The confidence might be part of her work frame of mind but work was a place where no one would dream of disputing the authority of someone like Luke Harrington.

Someone whose wrath was feared. You made sure children were where they were supposed to be when Mr Harrington was due for rounds. You picked up toys that could be tripped over. You made absolutely sure that any test results were available and you sympathised with the registrars and housemen who had to work to their utmost ability to win recognition from this perfectionist surgeon.

'You'll find something else is far more suitable,' Luke said firmly. 'A house that has adequate insulation and central oil-fired heating and plumbing that works, for instance.'

He was so confident. Standing there all dark and serious and so sure of himself. So far above Amy in any pecking order she could think of. It took courage to stand up to him.

'We can't afford to rent a house like that. Not big enough for all of us. Not in central London, that's for sure.'

'So move away from London, then. Surely a rural environment would be a better place to be running a…whatever the modern equivalent of an orphanage is?'

'A foster-home,' Amy responded quietly. 'And some of these children retain contact with their birth families. Kyra visits her mother every couple of weeks. She's hoping she can move home again one day. That contact would be lost if we moved away.'

Amy took a step closer. She had to make him see how important this was. Her voice rose but she was pleased to hear it gaining strength. 'We'd probably lose the children because Social Services tries to place them in a radius of their own homes for precisely that kind of reason. They need something familiar in their territory like a school. And besides…' Amy straightened her back and glared at Luke, outrage colouring her tone. 'This is my *home*. I came here to live when I was ten years old. When my dad died. Uncle Vanni was like a father to my sister and me. There's no way he would have wanted us to lose this house. There *is* another will. There *has* to be.'

'Arrangements are already in place,' Luke said with finality. 'The house is going to be demolished.'

'Over my dead body!' Amy snarled.

The surgeon was clearly taken aback by such blatant defiance. But then he simply turned away as though he couldn't see any point in continuing this discussion. He was avoiding eye contact. He didn't intend to be persuaded that any viewpoint other than his own might be legitimate.

'We're going to contest the will,' Amy added bravely. She stared at the vein on Luke's temple that had become suddenly more obvious. He had to be incredibly angry. Beside the vein, the tiny line of a scar ran from the side of his left eye upwards to disappear under the waves of dark hair. She'd never noticed that before, but why would she? The only times she had been this close to the surgeon had been when he'd been wearing a hat and mask.

'Have you any idea how horrendously expensive that would be?'

'We're getting legal aid.' Amy crossed her fingers behind her back. She *hoped* they were getting legal aid. 'And there's no way you can do anything about demolishing this house while we're still living in it and…and we're *not* moving.' She resisted the urge to add, *So there!*

That scar was disconcerting. The kind of scar that could be left from a long-ago injury. Clearly, her unexpected and unwelcome visitor was telling the truth but it begged the question of why Uncle Vanni had not known the truth.

Or had he?

Amy tilted her head just enough to be able to discern that scar again. Had Uncle Vanni been afraid of what might have been the result of an horrific head injury? Had the thought of trying to raise a disabled son alone been too much?

No. That didn't make sense because Uncle Vanni had devoted his life to helping other people's children. Including disabled children, like Summer. But, then, why had he stayed in London and not returned to his native country? Because he couldn't bring himself to get that far away from his son? It was confusing. Disturbing.

'My solicitor will be in touch. His name is Reginald Battersby.'

'I've met him.' Amy stepped sideways, trying to position herself between Luke and the door. She couldn't let him leave like this. Where had that ray of hope gone? He understood, didn't he? He'd protected the children by going along with her lie.

And what about that strange sensation she'd experienced when she had watched him listen to Summer's chest without the benefit of a stethoscope? To see his ear laid so gently on tiny, fragile ribs? The way his half-closed eyes had made the dark fan of his eyelashes and the shadowing of stubble on his jaw so much more noticeable. There had been more than hope in the curiously warm, fizzy sensation flooding Amy at that point. Trust had been mixed with hope, dammit!

What had changed while she had been upstairs? She couldn't have been that wrong, surely? What had she done to deserve having that newfound trust broken?

It wasn't fair.

More than that. It wasn't *right*.

'Why do you want to do this?' Amy demanded. 'What have you got against us?'

'Nothing. Until very recently I had no idea my…father was living here. Until today I had no idea who you were.'

That was a good way to fuel her anger. If he'd had no idea his father had lived here, it might explain why he'd never visited before, but she worked with this man, for heaven's sake. He'd bawled her out only days ago, but she hadn't been important enough for him to bother learning her name. Never mind what she'd seen with Summer. Luke Harrington was not a nice man.

Amy's control snapped. She was more than ready to go into battle to defend her family.

'It'll look good, won't it?' she said with deceptive sweetness. 'The photo in the papers with us all sitting in the street? Right before Christmas. In the *snow*. With Summer's oxygen cylinder. Millions of people will see that someone who's supposed to care about children doesn't really give a damn. Even about one of his own patients.'

Luke's face was grim. 'That isn't going to happen. Reginald is going to find suitable accommodation. For *all* of you.'

'In the same place? I doubt it. We stick together here,' Amy warned. 'And I also doubt that your Reginald has any idea about what's suitable. The man's as old as Methuselah. He probably thinks foster-children should be earning their keep sweeping chimneys.'

'Don't be ridiculous!'

But Amy was just warming up. 'And even if you don't give a damn about us, what have you got against this house? It's gorgeous! Early Victorian architecture that deserves to be preserved. A lot of people will be very upset when they learn it's going to be bulldozed. We'll probably get any number happy to chain themselves to the railings. The media will love that, too.'

'The house is falling down. It's not even safe!'

'It could be fixed.'

'It would cost a fortune.'

'From what I've heard, that's exactly what you've got sitting in the bank!'

Ooh, she'd stepped over the line now. Onto the kind of personal ground that hospital grapevines thrived on. Amy didn't need to see the dangerous glint in Luke's eyes to know that he would hate being the subject of gossip. She also had the distinct feeling she was going to regret this.

'What makes you think I'm planning to keep the proceeds from this property?' Luke snapped. 'Not that it's any of your damn business, but I intend to donate any profits to an appropriate charity.'

Amy's jaw dropped. He didn't need the money. He didn't want the house. He was planning to get rid of it and *give* the money away?

Why not just give the house away?

To *them*?

He had pulled his gloves and keys from a pocket of the black coat. He was ready to leave and he only had to step around Amy to reach the door. He began to do just that.

'W-wait,' she stammered. She needed to repair the damage she'd just done. To find a way to present their case calmly. To get down on her knees and beg if that was what it would take.

'What for?' The disgust in Luke's tone suggested that nothing Amy could say would be worth listening to.

'For...for...' For the children, Amy wanted to cry. For my mother and sister and grandmother. For *me*. But tears threatened to choke her words and she needed to think. To say something that would stop Luke walking out the door.

And in that tiny gap of time as she hesitated, a cold wind rushed into the room. There was a loud bang as the back door from the scullery to the garden slammed and then...

'*Zoe!*' Amy sucked in her breath at her babysitter's precipitous entrance.

The girl had obviously been running and now she stood there with her mouth opening and closing but no sound emerging as she tried to catch her breath. The anorak she was wearing had a ripped sleeve.

'Zoe?' This time Amy let her concern show. 'Is everything all right?'

'No!'

'What's wrong?'

'Bernie!'

'Bernie? As in your mum's boyfriend?'

'Yeah…' Zoe managed a deeper breath. ''Cept he's not just a boyfriend any more. He's a— What do you call it when you're gonna get married?'

'Fiancé?'

'Yeah. He's gonna move in and he says Monty's got to go.'

'What? Why?'

'He says he's just a smelly stray and he's too big and he costs too much to feed and he's…he's going to get *rid* of him!' Zoe burst into tears.

Amy gathered the girl into her arms. 'It's all right, *cara*,' she said, more than once because Zoe was crying too loudly to hear her. 'We'll sort it out.'

Turning her head, Amy could see that Luke had moved closer, reluctance and concern warring on his features. This girl was clearly in trouble. Possibly injured. As a doctor he had a duty to help.

As a man, he wanted nothing more than to turn and get out of this house.

Behind Luke, Amy could see the frightened faces of several children.

'It's OK,' she told them. 'Nothing for you guys to worry about.'

They continued staring.

'Kyra? It's time Chantelle was in bed and could you make sure the twins and Summer are OK? Give the boys a kiss for me. They're probably asleep by now.'

'But what's wrong with Zoe?'

Amy felt the girl shudder in her arms and a nose scraped painfully on her collar-bone as Zoe buried her face. No doubt this teenager was embarrassed to be seen like this by the younger children.

'She's upset,' Amy told them. 'But she's OK. Don't worry, I'm going to sort it out. You can help by getting yourselves off to bed.'

'But—'

'Come on.' Robert gave Amy a nod that said he could deal with this. 'Upstairs, all of you. Do what Amy says.'

'Thanks, Rob.'

The boy paused in the doorway, uncertainty in his face as he glanced back.

'We're OK,' Amy assured him. 'Mr Harrington's still here.'

Oh, God. He *was* still here. Was he ever going to be able to escape?

Not immediately, that was for sure. He could hardly walk out when this strange-looking girl was obviously in some sort of trouble with a soon-to-be stepfather. And what about that ripped jacket? How heavy handed was this Bernie character? Was it possible the confrontation had become physical? And who the hell was Monty? The girl's boyfriend? Brother?

She was just a kid. A weird-looking kid dressed completely in black, with jet-black hair that sported an electric pink streak and enough piercings to send a metal detector into overload. In the brief glimpse he'd already had, Luke had seen a ring through her lower lip, something in her nose and eyebrows and the ear that was currently visible had ornaments around its entire perimeter. Even through the tragus in the centre.

She was maybe sixteen years old? Young enough to be admitted to a paediatric ward in any case. Young enough to need protection. To deserve safety and assistance. If there was an angry man involved, he could hardly leave Amy and a bunch of vulnerable children to defend themselves, could he?

As fiercely as Amy had just demonstrated she was prepared to defend the people she cared about, she was just a slip of a woman herself. Delicate...physically, anyway. There was certainly nothing delicate about this woman's spirit.

The very thought of her having to defend herself physically was abhorrent. So much so that Luke had to take a deep breath to steady himself. He needed something else to focus on. Something real that couldn't stir imaginary and therefore useless emotional reactions.

'Can you get Zoe to sit down?' he suggested. 'We need to find out if she's been hurt.'

'I'm not *hurt*!' The girl pulled back from Amy's embrace. 'Bernie wouldn't hurt *me*.' Luke could see eyes that seemed disconcertingly pale thanks to thick black make-up that hadn't entirely run down the pale face. 'And I've hidden Monty so he can't do anything to him, either. Who're you?'

'This is Mr Harrington, Zoe,' Amy said. 'He's a surgeon at Lizzie's where I work.'

'What's he doing here?' Zoe's gaze flicked back to Amy. 'Is he your *boyfriend* now?'

'*No!*'

Did she have to sound quite that horrified? As though she wouldn't consider dating him if he were the last man on earth?

And why had Amy's face flushed so pink? Her eyes were so dark compared to the pale blue of Zoe's. Luke stared back at the two female faces. Dark eyes were *so* much more attractive, he found himself thinking and in that same moment he was horrified at himself.

Not because he considered Amy's eyes attractive but because something so shallow—so *emotional*—had actually distracted him so he wasn't thinking of anything else. Just the kind of mental behaviour he had conquered long ago.

What the hell was going on here?

'I'll explain later,' Amy told Zoe. 'Are you sure you're not hurt? Your jacket's all ripped…' She touched Zoe's cheek and Luke could swear he felt that touch himself.

So gentle. So full of genuine concern. It tugged at something deep within Luke. Something disturbingly poignant.

'I ripped the jacket on some wire in the shed. That's where I hid Monty.'

'It's too cold to leave him in there. You'll need to bring him inside.'

'He can come here?' Zoe's face brightened. 'You don't mind?'

'Of course not. We love Monty. We'll…adopt him.'

'What if Mum says you can't?'

'Do you think she would?'

'Nah. She'd be glad to get rid of him.' Zoe scrubbed at her nose and Luke winced at the thought of the metal spike in her nostril getting in the way. 'She wasn't that happy when I saved him from getting beaten up by those boys.'

'He's got a home here,' Amy said firmly. 'And you can visit whenever you want to. How much can it cost to feed one dog, after all?' With another squeeze of Zoe's shoulders and a discreet but anxious glance at her watch, Amy moved to the stove to pick up a kettle. 'Hot chocolate coming up,' she said cheerfully.

'I'll just go and get Monty,' Zoe said. 'And his blankets and stuff. Is that cool? I'll only be a few minutes.'

'Sure. But be as quick as you can. I can't be late for work.'

The cold-water tap over the old porcelain sink was turned on and a ghastly, shuddering noise filled the kitchen.

'Good grief,' Luke said. 'What is *that*?'

'Just air in the pipes,' Amy said offhandedly. 'It'll come

right in a tick.' Sure enough, the water spat and dribbled and then began to flow and the dreadful noise abated.

Luke opened his mouth and then shut it again. This was hardly the time to score further points about how inadequate this housing was. Not when Amy had just collected another inhabitant. Somehow it didn't surprise him that she would be prepared to lavish emotional energy on animals, as well as people. She was half-Italian, after all. Plenty of emotional energy to go around.

A heavy, unfamiliar feeling was gathering over Luke like dark clouds. He had known it would be a mistake to set foot in this house.

Amy seemed to be thinking hard, but Luke could read nothing in her expression when she glanced in his direction. She gave a slight nod just as the first tendril of steam escaped the spout of the kettle. Then she looked at her watch very deliberately.

'I absolutely have to go to work,' she said suddenly. 'I'll let Margaret know what's happening. She might be able to get a pool nurse in to cover and then I'd be able to come home.' Amy was speaking very fast, the words tumbling over each other. 'I've got my mobile. Could you please tell Zoe to text me if she needs me?'

'You can't leave!' Luke made the statement an order.

'I have to. I can't afford to lose my job.'

This was unacceptable. Luke stared at Amy. 'You're going to leave a house full of children? Unattended?'

'I'm not leaving them unattended,' Amy said calmly. 'You're here.'

'I'm not staying.'

'Why not? It's *your* house. And it's not for long. Zoe will be back in just a few minutes.' She sounded extraordinarily calm.

'I don't really see that you've got a choice, Mr Harrington. Sorry.'

She didn't *look* sorry. There was an expression curiously like satisfaction as Amy shrugged on a coat that hung behind the kitchen door, grabbed a bright red tote bag that stood beside the hutch dresser and practically ran from the house.

It all seemed to happen within seconds. Stunning! And now Luke knew what that strange, heavy feeling was.

Defeat. By stepping into this damned house he had stepped onto a battlefield and he had just lost the first skirmish. Something akin to admiration sneaked into the astonishment at the way he had just been manipulated.

Amy Phillips was certainly a force to be reckoned with.

There was no point continuing to stare at an empty doorway. Luke turned as the kettle began to whistle. He had to move to take it off the range and he was still standing there, lost in thought, when the back door opened again.

Zoe entered, holding a piece of rope. On the end of the rope was the biggest dog Luke had ever seen. Long, long legs and tufty hair and big sad brown eyes.

Luke stared. He couldn't help it. He knew he probably had an expression of extreme distaste on his face but he couldn't help that, either. He had a flash of sympathy for Bernie. This animal *was* too big and probably did smell and would, most likely, cost a fortune to feed.

'Don't worry,' Zoe told him scathingly. 'He probably doesn't like you, either.' She wrinkled her nose. 'I know who you are,' she informed him. 'And I *really* don't like you.'

'Oh?' Despite himself, Luke was curious. 'Why is that?'

'You made Amy cry.'

CHAPTER FOUR

THE route that cut through a corner of Regent's Park, crossed the busy main roads and then tracked past the ambulance entrance to Lizzie's emergency department had never been completed so fast.

Amy felt as if she was running for her life and her heart was still pounding so hard she had to slow down on the stairs up to the floor that housed the cardiology ward.

What had she done?

It had seemed like the perfect solution at the time. Of course the children couldn't be left without a responsible adult in attendance. Not when the babysitter was hardly more than a child herself and was currently distracted by her own problems.

Amy had taken a huge risk. She was banking on Luke Harrington's sense of duty being stronger than his desire to escape. She was also banking on nothing more than intuition, in the hope that she hadn't been wrong in sensing that he not only understood but was trustworthy.

She was forcing him to spend just a little more time in her household. Maybe enough time for him to think about what he intended to do and reflect on the effect it could have on the children he was—temporarily—responsible for.

But what if she was wrong?

What if he contacted Social Services or the police and reported a house full of abandoned children? A house that had sustained a small fire already that evening? Amy might arrive home to find they'd all been lifted from their beds and taken to places where they would be under more appropriate supervision.

She was good at texting as she moved. She fished her cellphone from the depths of her red bag.

'Zoe? U ok?'

'Al gud,' came the response. 'Talkin to G2.'

G2? Oh, *God!* Amy stopped on the landing between the first and second floors. She meant 'G squared'. Luke's nickname at Lizzie's. It stood for 'Grumpy Guts'. It hadn't occurred to Amy that the teenager would remember that, but there was nothing she could do about it now.

With a groan, Amy pushed up the last flight of stairs. She could only hope that Zoe wouldn't reveal her indiscretion to the head of Lizzie's cardiothoracic surgical unit.

'Do you know what they call you?' the girl said to Luke. '"G squared". It stands for "Grumpy Guts".'

'I beg your pardon?'

'Grumpy Guts,' Zoe repeated with relish. 'Nobody likes you. Not even Monty, and he likes everybody.'

Sure enough, the extraordinarily tall dog, who was now sitting on a patched old blanket, was giving Luke a steady glare that could only be described as menacing. If it started growling, Luke was out of there.

Zoe was watching him just as intently. Disconcertingly, only one eye was visible due to her strange, asymmetric fringe. 'Why don't you just go home?' she demanded.

Luke wasn't used to social interaction with teenagers and he had never been this close to one who looked quite like this. Was she a member of some cult? The absurdly immature response of '*This* is my home' occurred to Luke and he actually felt the corner of his mouth twitch. Instead, he shrugged off his coat, hung it over the back of a chair and sat down at the kitchen table.

'I'm not going anywhere,' he said calmly. 'I wouldn't dream of leaving a houseful of children with no adequate supervision.'

'Whaddya mean by that?'

'You're no older than the children you're supposed to be looking after.'

'I am so! I'm *sixteen*!' The single eye narrowed. 'Are you saying I'm stupid or something?'

Behind the aggressive response, Luke saw the fear that Zoe believed that might be true. Had somebody suggested it already or was this just the normal kind of low self-esteem teenagers could struggle with?

'Not at all.' Luke held her gaze. 'You've demonstrated you can cope very well. There's not many people that would rescue a wolf. Twice!'

Zoe was silent for a moment and then her mouth twisted into a grin that lit up her face. The delight was rapidly stifled, however.

'I still don't like you.'

Luke nodded. 'Because I made Amy cry.'

'Yeah.'

He frowned. 'I don't remember *seeing* her cry.'

''Course you didn't. She did it in the loo. She told me about it 'cos I was crying about something this chick at school said. Amy said it was good to cry but then you had to suck it up and get on with your life. You couldn't let mean things people said pull you down.'

'Mean things?' Luke was racking his memory. 'I don't say mean things to people.'

'You did. You told Amy she was stupid.'

'No.' The head shake was decisive. 'I would never say that.'

'You did!' Zoe insisted. 'It was in the middle of the night and this baby got real sick and it had to have a tube thing stuck into it and Amy was trying to help you and the baby was screaming and she tried to give it a cuddle and she touched the stupid tube and you yelled at her and told her she was stupid.'

Luke closed his eyes for a second. He remembered. About 3:00 a.m. last Thursday. He'd still been in the building due to emergency surgery on a child with major chest trauma from a car accident. An inpatient in the ward had run into trouble and needed a central line inserted. It had been a difficult enough procedure even getting local anaesthetic in place and then his nursing assistant had inadvertently brushed the sterile catheter with the sleeve of her gown.

'I didn't say she was stupid,' he said slowly. 'I think I said she was incompetent. That it had been a very clumsy thing to do.'

Zoe didn't answer. She was busy texting on her bright pink phone. Luke thought about the incident some more.

It had been a clumsy error and he'd been tired and concerned about the child he'd only just left in Intensive Care. And the nurse assisting him had been gowned and masked and gloved and…and he hadn't considered her feelings at all, had he?

The slip hadn't been a catastrophe. The trolley always had plenty of spare catheters and she had proved herself perfectly competent as she had silently continued to assist with the procedure. The knowledge that she had taken herself off afterwards to deal with the effects of his criticism came as something of a shock.

And 'Grumpy Guts'?

Yes, he avoided social interaction with his colleagues. And, yes, he expected others to try and meet the professional standards he set for himself, but he was always polite and fair and he gave praise whenever it was deserved.

He had made Amy cry.

Amy—who was brave enough to fight for her family. To comfort and protect anyone who was in trouble. Even a dog. Strong enough to go and do what she had to do even though she must have known it was a risk.

Had it not occurred to her that he could just call in some appropriate authority and have this household disbanded in one easy stroke?

Luke could still see the plea in those dark eyes when she had asked him not to reveal his real reason for being in the house. He remembered the smile and the way it had made him feel, and then he understood.

Amy was trusting him.

She may not like him any more than Zoe did but, for whatever reason, she had handed over the responsibility of something she cared about passionately. If he broke that trust, he could guarantee she would hate him for ever.

Luke didn't like that idea at all.

And it was only for an hour or two, wasn't it?

The ward was, mercifully, quiet.

Margaret was due to go home but she hadn't left yet. She was sitting in her office, gaping at Amy.

'Luke Harrington? In your house? *Babysitting?*'

'*His* house, apparently, and he wants to kick us all out onto the streets. Right before Christmas. Can you believe it?'

'No.' Margaret shook her head for emphasis. 'Why would he want to do something like that?'

'Because he's not a very nice man.'

'He's a lonely man,' Margaret said quietly. Her glance at Amy was a warning. 'Not that I'm one to gossip.'

'I know that.' Amy smiled at the senior nurse. 'And I'm sorry to dump on you, but I've got no one to turn to right now and I'm scared, you know? I can't let anything happen while Mamma and Rosa are away. These children are Mamma's life. They're part of our family.'

'I know.' Margaret leaned forward to pat Amy's hand. 'And I can help. Let's hope Personnel can come up with some cover for you tonight. If not, I'll stay on myself.'

'You can't do that. You'd be way over your hours.'

'Did you really leave Luke babysitting?'

'Kind of. I'm hoping he'll get a feel for the place and then realise how sad it would be to break up the family.'

Margaret's frown looked puzzled. 'I would have thought that would be the last thing Luke, of all people, would want to do.'

'Why do you say that?' And why had she described Luke Harrington as 'lonely'? The word was echoing in Amy's head.

Lonely people needed comforting.

They needed love.

'If I tell you something, will you promise it won't go any further?'

Amy nodded and Margaret lowered her voice. 'I grew up in Harrington Village,' she said.

'Oh-h-h!' Amy could feel her eyes widening. 'Where the

manor house is? And Mr Harrington's incredibly rich family?'

'You know about that?'

'I kind of guessed. It's why he's inherited the house. Uncle Vanni's wife was a Harrington. She died in a horrible car accident.'

'I heard that both Luke's parents were killed in a car crash.'

'It's obviously what they wanted people to think. Maybe Uncle Vanni wasn't considered good enough to be part of the Harrington clan.'

That was a possible explanation, wasn't it? That Uncle Vanni had said his son was dead because he'd been too mortified to confess he'd been deemed unacceptable?

Margaret was frowning. 'I don't know about that. What I do know is that my son went to school with Luke. He went to visit the manor house a few times. He said it was really scary.'

'Ghosts?' Amy was enthralled. She could picture a vast, old gloomy house with pictures of Luke's ancestors glowering down from within ornate gilt frames. A house that was hundreds of years older than the one she lived in and one that could have been the scene of feuds and scandals and possibly even murders....

But Margaret was shaking her head. 'Luke's grandmother.'

Amy blinked. OK, her nonna could be fierce and she had been known to poke an errant child with a knobbly finger or even her walking stick, but she was *family*. Family shouldn't be scary.

'She's a wonderful woman,' Margaret continued. 'She must be nearly ninety now but she's the guardian of just about every charitable trust in the district. I didn't exactly move in the same circles but I often saw her and she's the ultimate *lady*, you know what I mean?'

Amy thought of Luke. The way he chose his words and spoke so clearly. The way he dressed and his reputation as a surgeon with unparalleled skill and attention to detail.

Margaret lowered her voice to a whisper and there was a definite twinkle in her eyes. 'I wouldn't be the least bit surprised if Lady Harrington still wore corsets!'

Amy nodded slowly but her smile was distracted. She was beginning to understand. Luke had been brought up in an alien world and taught that everything had to be perfect. Lady Harrington wouldn't have considered there was space in that world for a foreigner. Especially an Italian with that reputation of volatility and exuberance the nationality carried.

Was it possible that Luke had been brought up to believe his father was dead? If that was the case, it would explain why no contact had ever been made. It would also mean that Luke would have been shocked to learn of his inheritance. Quite apart from a justified anger at a parent who had apparently chosen not to raise him, he was being left a dwelling in a state that was far from the perfection he'd been raised to expect.

No wonder his first reaction had been to consider demolishing it.

He'd never had a real family so he had no means to understand that it was what was within the walls of a dwelling that really mattered.

Maybe Luke was the one who was wearing a corset. An emotional one.

Amy got to her feet. 'I'm going to check on everybody on my list,' she announced. 'By the time I've done that, hopefully there'll be a pool nurse here and I can go home.'

She wanted to get home as soon as possible.

She knew how to fix this. There was a shining light at the

end of what had been shaping up to be a very dark tunnel. The shadowy shape still blocking that light was man-shaped but Amy wasn't the least bit deterred.

She could fix Luke Harrington, too, if he let her!

An hour had ticked past and Luke realised he'd missed his dinner, but he wasn't the least bit hungry.

He'd been sitting at the kitchen table since Zoe had disappeared to chivvy the older children to bed and to read a bedtime story to Chantelle. The big house was quiet and, uncharacteristically, Luke allowed himself to continue sitting in his somewhat dazed state. He hadn't noticed that Monty had slithered off his blanket at some point and was now under the table. It wasn't until he felt the weight of a large, black nose on the shiny leather of his shoe that he was aware of how close the giant dog had become.

He didn't want to antagonise the creature by shifting his toes. One chomp and that leather might not be enough protection. Zoe should be back shortly and the dog would be under control. Hopefully.

It was only partly due to Monty's breath on his ankle that Luke didn't feel alone. He didn't really need to hear the odd, muted bump or giggle from overhead, either, to remember how many occupants this house had. The feeling of their presence was everywhere.

Like a heartbeat.

Slow and steady. Different to when Amy had been in the house. She had an air of vibrancy that increased the beat. Gave it a few unexpected ectopics, even.

Luke found himself smiling unconsciously at the nice, cardiological analogy. Yes. The pulse of anything would increase and become a little erratic if Amy was around.

Especially when she was provoked. Her fierce words still rang in his ears.

Over my dead body!

A ridiculous thing to say. Over-emotional rubbish. Except that, at the time, he'd had the disturbing idea that she'd really meant it. She felt *that* strongly about it.

Had he—*would* he—ever feel that strongly about anything? Be prepared to lay his life on the line? To want something so badly that life would not be worth living without it?

Of course not!

But, curiously—and for the first time—Luke could feel envious of someone who did feel that way. Someone who could experience the euphoria of genuine passion. The notion was merely a flash, however. Easily pushed aside when recognised.

Passion denied rational thought. It involved lows, as well as highs. Misery that counterbalanced any happiness. An uncontrollable roller-coaster that Luke would never step onto because he was rational. He had to be. His career demanded it.

Why hadn't he used his rational intelligence and walked away from Amy's passionate outburst? He had certainly intended to. He knew there was no point talking to someone in that state and the only way forward was to create space until they calmed down.

She'd managed to get under his skin, though, hadn't she? Prodded some weak spot he hadn't known existed and he'd been sucked into responding. Worse, he'd lost it to the extent of revealing that he was planning to demolish this house out of spite and he didn't even intend to keep the proceeds.

Zoe would tell him it was a mean thing to do.

And, dammit! She would be right.

It wouldn't hurt to leave it for a few days, would it? Until after Christmas.

For Amy's sake.

Zoe eventually came back to the kitchen.

'Monty! Get back on your rug!' Zoe gave Luke a scathing glance as the dog wriggled backwards. 'You still here?'

'Apparently.'

'Robert said you were shouting at Amy before I got here.'

'I never shout. If anyone was raising their voice, that would have been Amy.' Luke frowned. How much had the other children overheard?

'Robert says you're gonna pull our house down.'

'*Your* house?'

Zoe flushed. 'Well, Monty lives here now and he's my dog.' Her voice rose defiantly. 'You know what one of my mum's boyfriends said to us once?'

'Um… No.'

'He had some stuff of Mum's he wanted to keep. Like CDs. *He* said "possession is nine tenths of the law".'

Luke sighed. 'The legal system doesn't see it quite like that, I'm afraid.'

Zoe snorted. 'I don't care. It worked for Wayne. He got to keep Mum's stuff. It'll work for us, too.' Her eye was an angry slit. 'You can sod off now. And when you're gone, we'll keep you out. You'll see.'

The confidence was impressive. Quite endearing, really, but misplaced. Zoe needed to learn to think things through.

'Maybe I won't go anywhere,' Luke suggested. 'I could just move in and then I'd have the nine tenths of the law. Ten tenths, if you consider that I'm legally the owner.'

'You can't do that!' Zoe gasped.

Luke raised an eyebrow. 'It doesn't seem a problem having extra people moving in around here, so why not? Uncle Vanni's room is empty.'

Zoe actually believed him.

How crazy was that? Luke had the weird notion that he'd fallen down a rabbit hole and landed in a parallel universe. That he could even pretend to be thinking of doing something that would give his grandmother cause to disown him was… Well, it was unthinkable.

Or it had been. Until now.

What was even worse was that there was something vaguely appealing about the absurd notion.

Zoe looked ready to cry again. Luke was about to reassure her when a small, pyjama-clad figure appeared in the doorway.

'Chantelle?' Zoe moved towards the younger girl. 'What's up, sweetie? I thought you were asleep.'

'I was.' Chantelle rubbed her eyes. 'Summer woke me up. She's making a funny noise.'

Luke's chair crashed over backwards due to the speed with which he got to his feet. Monty also rose and growled menacingly, but Luke ignored both events.

'Show me,' he demanded. 'Which is Summer's room?'

The 'funny noise' Summer was making was a distressed whimper on every outward breath. A tired sound, as though the effort was just too great.

Stepping into the room, Luke was instantly aware that it had the feel and even the smell of Amy. It was messy, with the clothes she had been wearing strewn over an unmade bed, but he barely registered a memory of how those jeans had clung to slim hips and how soft the woollen jumper had looked. The colours in the room were vibrant, with bright curtains and cushions. A faintly exotic scent that Luke couldn't place, along with the flickering light from a low-burning fire, brought the room to life.

It was an attractive, cosy space but even with the glowing coals the ambient temperature wasn't enough to account for the sheen of perspiration visible on Summer's dark skin.

He shook her shoulder gently. 'Summer? Wake up!'

The child didn't stir. Luke peeled the covers off the little girl and felt for her pulse. Her skin felt chilled and it took a moment to locate a pulse at all. When he did, Luke wasn't surprised to find it far too rapid and very weak. Her heart was failing and her blood oxygen levels were already too low to be compatible with consciousness.

'What's wrong with her?' Zoe asked from behind him.

'She's got a fever. Probably an infection of some kind.'

'Like a cold or something?'

'Yes.' It had come on very fast but Summer's immune system had already been compromised.

'Is she really sick?'

'Yes.' He couldn't be less than honest with Zoe. 'Could you call an ambulance, please? Tell them I'm here and I said it was urgent.'

Zoe hesitated in the doorway. 'She's not…going to *die*, is she?'

The tone was anguished. Something Margaret had said flashed into Luke's mind. Something about the children that ended up in the Phillips household being lucky.

No one else had wanted to care for this dying child but here she was clearly very much loved. Luke's own heart gave an odd squeeze.

'Not if I can help it,' he told Zoe sombrely. 'But we need to hurry.'

Robert took Zoe's place in the room a second later. He stared at Summer and then at Luke and his look was accusatory. 'I thought you were Summer's doctor.'

'I'm one of them.'

'So why can't you make her better, then?'

'It's not always possible to fix things, Robert.' He must know that, surely? If he was here in a foster-home, life had been a lot less than perfect so far for this boy.

'Well, it should be,' Robert muttered. 'It's not fair.'

He turned and walked away and Luke sighed. Of course it wasn't fair. Neither was it fair that he was made to feel so guilty. He did his best and he knew he did it better than most. He couldn't afford to feel guilty. A failure. And he wasn't, he knew that.

Luke also knew he was going to try harder than he ever had before for this particular little girl.

The benefit of the location being so close to St Elizabeth's made itself apparent in the speed with which the paramedics arrived.

'Are you going to be all right,' Luke asked Zoe, 'if I go to the hospital with Summer?'

'I'll look after her.' Robert had appeared again as Luke carried Summer to the waiting ambulance.

'Lock the doors,' Luke reminded them. 'And call the police if anything scary happens.'

'We'll call Amy,' Zoe said. As though that was all the back-up they could need.

'Text her now,' Luke said in parting. 'Let her know I'm bringing Summer in.'

Amy arrived in the emergency department of Lizzie's within ten minutes of the ambulance but already Summer was in the resuscitation area, hooked up to every monitor available and with an IV cannula taped into a vein on her arm.

Luke was there, bent over the unconscious child, a stethoscope in his ears.

'What's happened?' Amy tried to sound calm.

'She's in heart failure.' Luke straightened and nodded at the ED consultant. 'Fine crackles. Widespread. Bilateral. I think you're right. We've got an infection that's tipped her instantly into failure.'

'This is serious, isn't it?' Amy moved to the head of the bed, reaching out to touch Summer's forehead with a gentle stroke. She looked up and found Luke watching, his eyes dark. Intense.

She could read the answer to her query there, but she had already known that. She could also read a level of sympathy that came as a surprise. Again, she had the impression that Luke understood. More than he realised, perhaps. More than he would want to admit to, anyway. In response to his gesture, Amy moved to one side of the room.

'We're starting a dopamine infusion,' Luke told her, 'to combat the heart failure. We'll adjust her diuretics and add in spiranolactane. We'll also have a think about using an ACE inhibitor and beta blockade. We've taken bloods, of course, to try and isolate the precipitating infection, and we've already started her on antibiotics.'

'I should ring my mother. What time is it in Italy?' Amy looked at her watch, but then bit her lip. 'Maybe I should wait till morning. If I tell her now, she'll insist on heading home. Possibly with my grandmother in tow. That's not going to help anyone, is it?'

'What about consent?' Luke queried. 'We should talk about how you feel about mechanical support, like ECMO or a ventricular assist device.'

Amy stared at the surgeon. He was talking about extraordinary measures to keep Summer alive. ECMO delivered oxygen and removed carbon dioxide via catheters placed directly in a patient's heart and arteries. The ventricular device was only a little less invasive, with a device placed inside the heart to assist pumping. There were big risks associated with these therapies and they were only temporary. A lot of surgeons would argue there was little point in heroic attempts to keep Summer alive if it only delayed the inevitable.

Luke seemed to be reading her thoughts. 'It might buy some time,' he said quietly. 'I can't promise anything.'

But he looked as if he'd *like* to promise something, and Amy smiled. He might try to hide it but—underneath the armour—there was a man who really cared. Not someone who could throw a bunch of children out of their home.

'We should talk,' she agreed. 'As far as medical consent goes, I signed up as a carer for Summer along with my mother. I have the authority to sign any necessary consent forms.'

'What would you like me to do?'

'Whatever you can.' Amy's lip trembled. 'I know it's a lot to ask, but it would be so special if we can have Summer with us for Christmas.'

Luke gave a single nod, as though he had expected the response. He moved to talk to the ED staff.

'Let's get Summer up to the ICU.' He sought Amy's gaze as preparations were made. 'Are you coming?'

'Yes, of course.'

'We'll talk later, then, when we've got her settled and stable.'

A little over an hour later, Amy sat beside Summer's bed in the intensive care unit, holding her small hand.

'She's holding her own,' Luke decided, looking up from a printout of test results. 'Her arterial blood gas levels are as good as we could expect. Her blood pressure's up and her heart rate and temperature are down.' He frowned at Amy. 'You should get some rest. I spoke to the night supervisor and your shift in the ward is covered for the rest of the night.'

'I need to stay with Summer.'

'She's going to sleep for hours yet. And you know how good the staff are in here.'

Amy did know. She also knew that Summer was so used to being in hospital that she probably wouldn't even be frightened. But what if something happened?

'Nothing's going to happen,' Luke said. 'Not in the next few hours.'

How could he read her mind like that? Amy dragged her startled gaze from Luke's face back to Summer's. She looked as though she was sleeping peacefully now and those dreadful noises of respiratory distress had almost gone.

'You might be needed at home,' Luke added. He cleared his throat when Amy didn't respond immediately. 'I got the impression that some of the other children were very worried about Summer.'

'They'll be worried sick,' Amy agreed. 'I tried to text Zoe but she's not answering. Hopefully, they're all asleep, but still…' She glanced at her watch. 'Good grief, it's nearly 2:00 a.m.!'

'And I need to collect my car. I'll walk you home.'

No! a voice in Amy's head cried in alarm. A walk in the middle of the night, alone with Luke Harrington? How terrifying would that be?

The stumble of her heart felt like someone thumping her

from the inside. Wake up! it conveyed. What better opportunity could you have to talk to him?

To plead her case?

He had helped Summer, hadn't he? He was prepared to go to extraordinary lengths to keep their little girl alive.

Surely, surely he could be persuaded that Summer—and the other children—needed their home just as much?

'OK,' Amy said bravely. 'I'll grab my stuff from the ward and meet you outside ED in five minutes.'

CHAPTER FIVE

'You look like a dragon.'

'Pardon?' Was this going to be another insight into what the staff of Lizzie's considered a less than amenable personality? 'Oh…!' Luke breathed out again and noted the white billow of his breath in the icy air.

Amy looked nervous. Was she expecting flames, as well?

'Where's your coat?' Amy was wrapping her own around her body more securely.

'Hanging over a chair in your kitchen.'

'But you can't walk home without one! You'll get hypothermia.'

'It's only a few minutes. I'll survive.'

Amy looked doubtful. 'We could call a taxi.'

'Could be a long wait. Besides, I could do with some fresh air and we need to talk.'

'Mmm.' He could see the way Amy sucked in a deeper breath. 'Right. About the house.' She set off as though keen to get it all over with.

Luke caught up within a couple of strides. 'Yes. Amongst other things.'

'Other things?' Amy latched on to a change of subject eagerly. 'Such as?'

'Summer.'

'Oh…' They turned to walk through the car park and Luke could see the top of Amy's head beside him, her dark hair hidden beneath a bright, rainbow woollen beanie. 'It's not looking good, is it?'

'No, I'm afraid not.'

'And she was well down the transplant list last time we heard.'

'I'll call the co-ordinating centre first thing tomorrow morning and see how she's placed at the moment.'

'Will you?' Amy's eyes shone as she looked up at him. 'Oh, thank you!'

Luke was getting that weird feeling again. Like he'd had when he'd gone along with that lie about why he had come to the house and Amy had smiled at him. The feeling of being powerful and generous even when he wasn't doing anything worthy of gratitude. It was less weird this time, though.

Pleasant, even.

'These lists can change dramatically. Sadly, a lot of children die while they're waiting.'

Amy sighed, her breath making a huff of vapour, the sadness of the sound chasing that pleasant sensation away. Luke wanted it back. She needed comfort of some kind but touching his companion in any way would not be appropriate so Luke stomped on the odd inclination to put an arm around her shoulders.

'Maybe Summer will be one of the lucky ones.'

'I hope so.' They waited at the side of the main road for a black cab to pass. 'It's awful to be wishing tragedy on another family, though.'

The taxi was gaily decorated with tinsel around the inside of its windows. Laughing passengers were wearing Santa hats.

'Especially at Christmas,' Amy added.

It was Luke's turn to sigh. 'It's just another day in the year, you know. The hype is out of all proportion if you ask me. I hate the way it becomes almost impossible to get things done.'

Like demolishing a house?

'And for what?' he added hurriedly, to drown out the un-invited voice. 'A commercial opportunity that's completely out of control.'

They were on Albany Street now, almost into the park, but Amy had slowed down. Virtually stopped. She looked horri-fied.

'But…but Christmas is *magic*!'

'You don't really believe that, do you?'

Stupid question. He could see she believed it. Her shining eyes and parted lips were illuminated by a streetlamp. She was practically *glowing*!

And…beautiful.

Amy Phillips was absolutely, stunningly…*beautiful*.

'Of course I do,' she said. 'It's the only time we all get to celebrate how important we are to each other. Oh, I know there's birthdays and Mother's Day and everything but Christmas is for whole families. For *everybody*! Neighbours and nurses and taxi drivers and…and even dogs.'

Luke was trying to get past the realisation of how stunning this woman was. How could he have never noticed before? He must have heard her voice with that tiny catch of exotic pronunciation even if he hadn't experienced the suggestion of huskiness that came with a subject she felt intense about. He must have seen that smile—the way it curled up at the edges and reached right into her eyes. Those *incredible* eyes! Had he been completely blind?

'Especially for the children,' Amy continued. 'It's magic

because they believe it's magic. The world is full of secrets and pretty decorations and special food and they get something to look forward to. To dream about.'

Unconsciously, Luke was shaking his head. Not all children. Not in the way Amy wanted to believe. Trapped deep inside himself was the echo of a four-year-old boy who had begged Father Christmas for a real family. One with a father and a mother and...*please*...a brother to play with.

'Ho, ho, ho,' Santa had chortled. He'd patted the little Luke on the back, firmly enough to encourage him to slide off his knee, and then he'd presented him with a lollipop.

A red one that was never eaten.

'I know...' Amy's expression had become anxious as she watched Luke's face. She started walking again and their feet crunched on frozen puddles on the path. Bare branches made an archway that drew them forward into the night. 'But it's like anything in life, isn't it? You can choose whether you focus on the good stuff or the bad stuff.' She smiled winningly up at Luke. 'What's that saying? Something like, "Life shouldn't be measured in how many breaths you take but by the moments that take your breath away"? Well, there's lots of those moments at Christmastime. *That's* what makes it magic.'

There was a plea in her face now. She wanted him to agree with her. It seemed terribly important that he should agree but Luke couldn't find a thing to say. He was having trouble catching his breath. Maybe it was one of those moments she was talking about but it had nothing to do with the time of the year and everything to do with Amy Phillips.

The path had the odd tree root sneaking along its edge and, because Amy's head was still tilted upwards as she appealed to Luke, she stumbled a little when her foot caught. Just enough to make it an automatic action on Luke's part to catch her arm and prevent her falling. She turned swiftly and, just as naturally, he caught her other arm and there she was—standing so close he could feel her warmth. Feel the almost desperate plea in her eyes.

She wanted something from him but Luke couldn't, for the life of him, concentrate enough to remember what it was.

Her closeness and the feel of her in his hands was mesmerising. In his experience, women who were in such close physical proximity and had a look on their faces even remotely like this wanted something he rarely had the time or inclination to bestow.

This time, however, he had no hesitation at all. It required no more thought than stealing that photograph had.

Luke bent his head and kissed Amy.

It was, absolutely, the last thing Amy had expected.

The conversation about Christmas had been the perfect lead in to presenting her case about the house but instead it had led to him intending to kiss her!

Here they were, on the outskirts of a huge, deserted, dark, frozen park in the middle of the night and Luke Harrington was going to kiss her!

Luke Harrington!

She should run. Physically and emotionally.

Life was way too complicated already.

Amy was poised to flee—every cell in her body charged with adrenaline—the choice between fight or flight made in the split second she saw the intention in Luke's eyes.

But then the distance between them closed and she could feel the warmth of his breath on the chilled skin of her face. She could *smell* him. A mix of potent masculinity and sheer power. She tried to run, at least mentally, but the instant Luke's lips touched hers, Amy tripped and fell headlong.

Into the kiss.

His lips felt cold and her own were more than half-numb but still this kiss felt like nothing she had experienced before.

It all happened so fast and Amy still had the sensation that she'd lost her balance and was falling, so she really had no choice but to reach out for something to hold on to. The solid chest in front of her was like a wall and her hands slid upwards, searching for an anchor. Luke's neck. Perfect.

So was the way his arms came around her body so securely. Safely. Counterbalancing the firm pressure from his mouth. With the fear of falling removed, Amy could relax just that fraction. Her lips parted just that fraction, as well, and the warmth of their breaths mingled and then there was *heat*.

Searing heat as Luke's tongue touched hers and Amy was falling all over again because the muscles in her legs were melting from that heat. Christmas decorations had nothing on the swirl of colours and sensations coursing through her entire body. Everything was melting, especially that core deep within her belly. The widespread, delicious tingle was changing shape, curling up at its edges and turning in on itself to make a hard knot of desire.

This wasn't simply a kiss.

It was an awakening.

A much less pleasant kind of awakening occurred when the kiss finally ran its course and they both stepped apart.

Luke looked as stunned as Amy felt and the chill of the night had increased dramatically. How long had they been standing, locked in each other's arms?

With a final, faintly shocked glance at each other, they continued walking. Silently.

Was Luke trying to absorb the startling effect of that kiss, as she was? She couldn't resist a tiny glance up at his face. If he hadn't believed in magic before, surely he was at least giving it some head room right now?

It was only a short distance from the tree beneath which they'd been kissing to the house on Sullivan Avenue, but if Luke had been as unaware as Amy of his feet actually touching the ground, he was giving no sign of it. When he eventually spoke, it was to express disbelief certainly, but the tone suggested anything but pleasure.

'Unbelievable!' The word was outraged.

The tension in the tall body beside Amy gave out vibrations that she responded to automatically. It was a rather similar sinking sensation to the one she'd experienced the other night, when she'd known she'd just touched a sterile object and brought a critical medical procedure to a screaming halt.

'What's wrong—?' Amy had to stop herself adding his name. It felt like it would be natural to call him Luke, but she couldn't, could she? And she could hardly call him Mr Harrington now. Not after he'd just kissed her so thoroughly!

Amy was following his line of vision even as the confused thoughts were jumbling in her mind. She could see his car. A gorgeous, low-slung, sporty model in an unusual shade of smoky blue.

Very low slung.

'Oh, no!' Amy breathed. Both the tyres she could see were as flat as pancakes.

Two brisk strides took Luke to the other side of his vehicle.

'Four flat tyres! This is deliberate vandalism,' he pronounced. His gaze snapped in two directions as he scanned the rest of the street. 'And mine seems to have been the only vehicle targeted.' He glared at Amy. 'I wonder why?'

'It does stand out,' she ventured. 'It's the only convertible and the colour is unusual.'

Luke said nothing and Amy squirmed inwardly. Oh, Robert, she thought in dismay. This was *so* not the way to express antagonism.

'Let's go inside, shall we?' Luke suggested dryly. 'I need to call a cab.'

He should have been as mad as hell about what had been done to his car.

Curiously, he actually experienced a flash of something that felt like gratitude for an excuse to follow Amy back into that house.

To stay close to her for just a little longer.

Luke was feeling slightly dizzy again. The way he had when Margaret had told him the house was full of children and Italian women. As though the very foundations of his world were being rocked.

And so they were.

It might have started when he'd recognised how attractive Amy was but the Richter scale had increased exponentially with that kiss.

Luke was feeling things right now that he had absolutely no experience with.

Intense, dangerous things.

They led to a place he'd never ventured into because he'd learned long ago that, if you were self-disciplined enough, you could keep yourself safe from that dangerous place.

Safe from nasty things. Boarding school had cemented

that lesson. And he'd already known that things that were *too* nice were also to be avoided. The hedonistic pleasures that were the stuff of irrational desires and behaviour. The benefits of a lifestyle that kept you safe from those places had been breathed in with the very air of his childhood.

Could he distract himself now?

Possibly.

Did he want to make any effort to do so?

No. Not just yet, anyway.

How could he, after *that* kiss? He was bewitched by a combination of the bizarre events that had unfolded since he'd left work for the day. It would wear off. Daylight would dispel the feeling of unreality. Even electric light might help.

Amy pulled off her woolly hat when they were inside the kitchen again. Wisps of dark hair escaped the plait and curled around her race, still picking up the inadequate light from the single bulb enough to gleam. Then she poked up the inside of the range, adding more fuel, and the fire tinged her face with a rosy glow.

Extra light wasn't helping. Luke's fingers were coming back to life now, stinging and burning at their tips. His lips had a similar tingling going on but he knew that wasn't from the recent, subzero environment. They were remembering that extraordinary kiss.

Wanting more.

'Sit down,' Amy invited. 'You must be totally frozen. I'll make some hot chocolate.' She put the kettle onto the stove and then moved to pick up another object as she walked towards Luke. 'Here's the phone. Why don't you call for a taxi while I just check on the children?'

She was back within a couple of minutes. 'They're all sound asleep,' she reported. 'Zoe's crashed in my bed so I'll use Uncle Vanni's room for the rest of the night.' She busied herself making a hot drink, spooning chocolate powder into mugs, wrapping a cloth around the handle of the kettle before pouring the boiling water and then opening a refrigerator to extract a carton of milk.

Ordinary movements but Luke found himself watching as though she was performing a magic show.

'Will the taxi be very long?' she asked.

'I haven't called them yet.'

She almost spilt the mugs of hot chocolate as she carried them to the table. She set them down carefully but the wobble in her voice gave away her nervous reaction.

'How come?'

'I want to talk to you.'

Amy sat down. She put her hands around her mug as though she needed the comfort of its warmth. She hung her head, pretending to inhale the rich aroma.

'The house,' she said finally.

Luke couldn't resist the opportunity. 'Amongst other things.'

Sure enough, her face lifted and he got a clear view of her eyes. The connection he was looking for caught instantly and, for a moment, Luke just went with it—torn between amazement and being appalled at the power he could sense.

Another dimension was there. Just waiting for him to step into it and to take that first step. All he needed to do was make physical contact. He could reach out and cover one of Amy's hands with his. Or stand up and pull her into his arms. Feel the…

'O-other things?' Amy's voice had a strangled quality.

With enormous difficulty, Luke broke the pull of the eye contact and stifled the first response that came to mind. The desire to talk about that kiss. About whether it had had the same kind of effect on her as it had done on him. About whether she would be interested in… *Hell*, he couldn't go *there*, could he?

Not with the obstacle of the intentions with which he had come to this house. He needed to ground himself. To remember why his life had intersected with Amy's in the first place.

'Tell me about your Uncle Vanni,' he commanded.

That should do it. He could listen to an account of his father's life. A happy life, no doubt, that had never included his own son. Involuntarily, Luke's gaze slid sideways—to where the flap of his coat hung around the back of the chair. To the pocket hiding that stolen article.

'Poor Uncle Vanni,' Amy said softly. 'He never recovered from losing the love of his life. *Both* of them, in fact.' Her gaze was accusing.

Luke could feel the hairs prickling on his neck again—the way they had when he'd seen that photograph. He was staring at a can of worms here and Amy had her hand on the lid, so to speak. Did he really want her to open it?

'What do you mean?' he asked, his voice harsh. 'Women?'

Amy shook her head. 'There was only ever one woman for Uncle Vanni. The other love of his life was his son. You.'

Luke couldn't meet her gaze. He didn't believe it. He couldn't afford to. It was doing more than rocking the foundations of his world. This had the potential to rip deep, dangerous crevasses in those foundations.

'Tell me,' he commanded gruffly. 'The story as you heard it.'

'OK.' Amy took a deep breath. 'Uncle Vanni fell madly in love with Caroline. He was working in a vineyard at the time, in northern Italy, and Caroline had been sent to this posh finishing school nearby. She was only eighteen and she had to go home but then she discovered she was pregnant and all hell broke loose.'

Luke found himself nodding slowly. He could imagine how that news would have gone down. His grandmother would have considered her daughter's life ruined.

'Caroline ran away,' Amy continued. 'Back to Italy. She married Uncle Vanni and they had a gorgeous baby and they were blissfully happy, even though they didn't have much money.'

They had certainly looked blissfully happy in that photograph.

'So what happened?'

'There was a dreadful accident. Their car was really old and the brakes failed on a mountain road. They were all badly injured. Caroline died just a few hours later and Uncle Vanni was evacuated to a big hospital in Milan. He was in Intensive Care for weeks and in the hospital for nearly six months. It was two years before he could work again and he had trouble with his back and feet for the rest of his life. Lived in slippers did Uncle Vanni.'

Luke pushed the image of those comfortable slippers from his mind. Then he cleared his throat.

'And…and the baby?'

'Caroline had her passport because they had been planning to cross the border at some point. They'd been married for three years or so by then but were going on their first real holiday. Anyway, the hospital and the police tracked down her family and her mother apparently arrived the next day. She arranged a medical escort and took both the baby and Caroline's body back to England.'

'And then?' Luke had to clench his fists to stop himself touching that scar beside his left eyebrow.

'It was months before Uncle Vanni was fit to travel but as soon as he could, he came to England to try and find his son.' Amy raised her eyes to Luke's and he could see the moisture shining in them. Could hear the catch in her voice that seemed to be attached by an invisible sting to his own heart. It tugged.

'Do you know, even more than thirty years later, Uncle Vanni couldn't talk about any of this without breaking down? He was in a really bad way when he got to this country. Broken in body and spirit. It took huge courage to go to Caroline's home and face her mother and when he did, he was told that his son's injuries had been too severe. Despite the best medical care the Harringtons could access, that little boy had died a week or so after they brought him back.'

Luke's mouth opened. He snapped it shut again. What could he say? Amy was clearly telling the truth as she knew it. What good would it do to tell her that his grandmother valued honesty above everything?

'He never went back to Italy. For a few years he just existed in London. He had a job as a school caretaker and he lived in a bedsit in some horrible high-rise. My mother found him when we came to live in London and he gradually became part of our family.' Amy took a deep breath and then gave her head a tiny shake. 'Anyway… My dad was a policeman and there was a job one night when these kids had to be taken into care. There was a big mix-up and Dad ended up bringing them home for the night. The youngest was a boy who was about three years old and he homed in on Uncle Vanni and climbed up on his knee. Looking back, I suspect that was the turning point but unfortunately things got worse before they got better.'

'How so?'

'My dad got killed on duty. Shot. I was nine. Mum was

going to pack us all up and move back to Italy, but she's never been very good at making decisions and then acting on them. She had to rely on Uncle Vanni and he finally started to come out of the depression he'd been struggling with for so long. And then he got the "great idea".'

'Which was?'

Amy stopped and took a sip of her drink and then continued. 'He decided that if his own son was lost to him, rather than waste the rest of his life, he'd spend it looking after children that other people didn't want. But he couldn't do it by himself. He needed my mother as part of the family to get approval to be a foster-parent himself. He found this house and persuaded her to stay at least for a while and that's where it all started. It's been my life ever since.'

'But your uncle's dead now.'

'My mother is just as passionate about these children as he was. When he was dying, she promised she would look after them as if they were her own. And they are, really. She loves them. We all love them.'

'So why didn't he do something about protecting them? Legally?'

'You mean, the will? I have my own theory about that.' Amy's smile was poignant.

'Which is?'

'Uncle Vanni was a wonderful man. He'd do anything for anyone, but he wasn't perfect by any means and he had a bad habit of convincing himself that he'd done things because he had intended to do them.' Amy stuck her tongue into her cheek as she pondered and Luke felt an odd twist in his gut as he watched.

'Like—he'd be given a chore like posting a letter or taking out the rubbish and he'd say he'd done it. And then, when he was asked if he'd done it, he'd sneak off and actually get it done before he got caught out. I was there once when he put his hand in his pocket and found a letter he'd forgotten to post and he winked at me, like it was our secret. The thing is, he was a hopeless liar. The real secret was that we all knew. Asking him if he'd done something was just a reminder but he would always say he'd done it because he didn't like to let anyone down and he always *intended* to do it.'

'So you think he intended to make a new will and didn't get around to it.'

Amy nodded. 'And nobody would have reminded him because anything to do with death was so upsetting for him. It would remind him of what he'd lost. Maybe that was the reason he couldn't bring himself to actually go and do it. Or maybe he just kept putting it off, telling himself there was plenty of time.'

'Only there wasn't.'

'No. It was so sudden. A massive stroke. They kept him on life support for a couple of days but then we had to let him go.'

Luke was silent. He was struggling with this. Clearly, Amy believed she was telling the truth. The story rang with the resonance of truth and he could sense that faded photograph hidden in his coat pocket. The evidence all around him supported Amy's account. And 'Uncle Vanni' had been a hopeless liar, so he must have believed he was telling the truth.

But if it *was* true, it went against everything Luke had been brought up to believe was true, and it threatened to cut deeply into the respect he had for the woman who'd raised him.

Things that had been so black and white—like the values he'd based his life on—were being held up for inspection and, instead of the solid foundation he'd believed them to be, they were shaky.

Flawed?

Luke didn't like that notion. It would mean that a part of himself was potentially just as flawed, and he wasn't ready to accept that.

He got slowly to his feet. 'I don't think I'll bother waiting for a taxi,' he said. 'I'll walk.'

'Is it far?'

Far enough to give him time to think, at least. Luke put his coat on. He picked up his scarf and gloves. 'I won't get cold this time.'

Amy went to the door with him. She seemed tired, which was hardly surprising given that it was after 3:00 a.m. now, but it was more than that. She was sad. Did she miss the father figure she'd had in her life?

At least she'd known him.

'You need to rest,' Luke told her.

They were close again. Too close. The temptation to kiss her again enveloped Luke with painful intensity.

'I will,' Amy said. 'I'll call Lizzie's first, though, and see how Summer's doing.'

'I'll check on her first thing. I'll be back at work by 6:00 a.m.'

'Maybe you should just stay here. You're not going to get much sleep after walking home.'

'I might go back to Lizzie's and use the on-call room.' The temptation was strangling Luke. He couldn't stay here and keep his hands off this woman.

But he had to pause, once more, as he stepped out into the night because the soft sound of Amy's voice was arresting.

'He did love you,' she said quietly. *'Luca.'*

There it was again. That name. That pronunciation. Pulling him…somewhere.

Somewhere he couldn't go because he had no idea how to get there.

And it was too disturbing.

'Did you really have no idea?' Amy asked.

'No.' Luke could hear the trace of bewilderment in his own voice. 'No idea at all.'

CHAPTER SIX

'CHRISTMAS shopping, was it?'

'Sorry?' Luke turned on the water and picked up the small brush to start scrubbing in. It was 6:30 a.m. and the question from his registrar was baffling.

'That huge carton I saw you coming out of the lift with. You looked as if it was something you were planning to hide.'

'Mmm.' Maybe he'd looked as furtive as he'd felt. Luke hoped he hadn't been observed earlier, down in the bowels of St Elizabeth's Hospital, following the directions of that co-operative cleaner to where the recycling and large items of rubbish were collected. 'Definitely Christmas stuff,' he said in a tone that would discourage any further questions.

'Great time of year, isn't it?' his registrar said cheerfully. 'Rather fun, hiding stuff and surprising people.'

'Mmm.' Luke paid careful attention to scrubbing beneath his nails. His registrar should know he wasn't one for idle chitchat right before surgery when his focus was on what lay ahead. He certainly didn't want to start thinking about that early morning mission because then he would start thinking about Amy. Wondering how he could present that box of decorations currently sitting in a corner of his office. Imagining the sparkle of pleasure he might see in her face.

And if he started to think about that, his mind would latch back on to what had kept him largely awake for the few hours he'd spent in the single bed the on-call room boasted. Back to that kiss. The way he had felt holding Amy in his arms. That spiral of desire—or was it actually *need*?—had to be firmly damped.

The bright lights of the operating theatre suite should be far more effective than daylight even in restoring reality, and Luke would welcome the return to normality. He could hasten it, by a nudge in the right direction.

'So you know what's on the agenda this morning? For baby Liam?'

'Three surgeries in one go, from what I could gather.'

'Pretty much. An arterial switch, VSD closure and repair of an aortic coarctation.'

His registrar whistled silently and any thoughts of Christmas shopping were clearly dispelled. They were in for a long, hard session in Theatre.

Preparations to put the infant onto the heart-lung bypass machine were painstaking and time-consuming, complicated by having to leave access to the arteries that needed repositioning. It was nearly 8:00 a.m. when the tiny heart was stopped with the cold, high-potassium solution that would also protect the heart muscle while it was not functioning.

Luke was already deep within the zone that would enable him to operate with no lessening of precision for many hours. Cutting tiny areas of miniature vessels and placing stitches he needed magnifying goggles to visualise accurately. Coating every suture line with fibrin glue.

Short breaks to flex muscles and counteract strain were taken, but for minimal periods of time only. Six hours on bypass were getting to the limits of what a baby could tolerate well and Luke intended finishing before then.

The session finished, as it had begun, with another complication. An abnormal rhythm persisted after the heart was restarted and did not respond well enough to the cocktail of drugs Luke ordered.

'We'll keep him ventilated and on sequential atrioventricular pacing,' he decided eventually. 'Let's get up to ICU.'

Had he bothered to think about it, Luke would have decided he was entirely grounded in reality again by the time he accompanied his patient to the highly specialised unit. The fact that nothing remotely unprofessional crossed his mind made it a non-issue.

So it was a huge shock to walk into the unit and see Amy sitting beside Summer's bed, holding the little girl's hand. Leaning forward to press a gentle kiss to her forehead.

To instantly remember his own experience of the touch of Amy's lips.

And—ever so slightly—to feel the ground shift beneath his feet once more.

'It's Christmas Eve tomorrow,' Amy was telling Summer. 'When all the boys and girls are asleep, Father Christmas will come and leave presents under the tree.'

'For…me?'

'Of course for you, darling.' Amy kissed Summer's forehead. 'I'll bring it in when I come to visit.'

She looked up, aware of the activity beyond the glass windows of Summer's cubicle, in time to see the surgical team come past with a tiny, post-operative patient that had to be baby Liam. It was no surprise that the baby's surgeon was still close by.

What *was* surprising enough to take Amy's breath away was the way her heart seemed to stop and her skin come alive so that every cell tingled. The way she felt a connection to this man that went far deeper than any she had the right to feel.

They had shared a kiss, that was all.

One kiss.

It was nonsense to feel as though so much more than their lips had touched. As though their souls had made contact. Maybe it was the result of over-thinking, which was a trait Amy was sure she had inherited or learned from her mother. The ability to endlessly replay and examine tiny snatches of life. To experience them again and again. To analyse them and consider every possible repercussion.

The way Amy had done only last night after Luke had gone. As she'd lain, wakeful, in Uncle Vanni's bed.

For a while she'd simply remembered—and missed—the person who'd been the most important man in her life for so many years. It had been a natural progression of her thoughts to realise that Uncle Vanni had, indirectly, been responsible for bringing a new man into her life.

Her mother would have probably proclaimed that it was meant to be and given thanks to some obscure saint.

Amy was fighting the same tiny voice in her own head that was saying the same thing. The one that was noting every re-action she had to Luke Harrington.

The one that was taunting her with the accusation that she was falling in love.

Amy had done her best to argue back.

Don't be ridiculous. He's from another planet.

He's a man, the voice whispered back. *You're a woman.*

He's rich. Incredibly rich. I wouldn't even know what spoon to use if he took me out to dinner.

But you want *him to take you out to dinner.*

No! It could never work.

Why not?

He's important. I'm…nobody.

Really?

Not according to the way he judges people. I'm nothing. Just a nurse. He couldn't even remember my name.

I'll bet he remembers it now. After that kiss.

Ah, yes… That kiss.

And the voice had an argument compelling enough to almost obliterate any arguments Amy's rational side could muster.

Remember what Margaret said? He's lonely.

It struck something nameless and deep and Amy suspected that's what the connection was all about. Yes, she and Luke came from totally different worlds and it might be far too great a challenge to understand and appreciate what was most important in each other's lives, but that could be part of the connection because Luke might not even realise how lonely he was.

He obviously hadn't had any idea his father had loved him and Amy wasn't sure that her heartfelt story last night had convinced him. He needed convincing if she was going to change his mind about the house.

He also needed—as everyone did—to be loved.

And that was something that Amy did have. Surely the ability to love transcended the barriers of status and wealth?

At some point during the remaining hours of darkness and internal conversation, an idea had been born.

A plan.

And while Amy's first objective in coming to Lizzie's this afternoon had been to spend some time with Summer, she had also been planning to see Luke. To talk to him. To offer up her plan.

There was an awful lot resting on his acceptance of that plan, so it was no wonder she was nervous. No wonder that her heart tripped and accelerated when she saw him. Not that it could explain why it was so hard to look away from him but the eye contact didn't last long enough to be an issue.

Luke was busy. She could see him supervising the transfer of the baby to the care of the unit staff. Consulting with the other specialists who came in. Making final adjustments to the life-support equipment and finally, taking a phone call.

When he caught her gaze on terminating the call, Amy had the horrible impression he had been aware of how often she had been looking in his direction. As though he had expected to make eye contact the second he had chosen to look *her* way.

Just as he expected her to respond to the subtle movement of his head that was an invitation to leave Summer's side and join him.

'Be back in a minute, sweetheart,' she murmured. The reassurance was more for herself than Summer, who seemed to be sound asleep again.

Could Luke feel that disturbance in the air that intensified with every step closer that she took? A feeling of…awareness was the only description she could come up with. She was *so* aware of everything about this man.

She'd seen in him in scrubs before, of course, but this was completely different because this time it was in the wake of having been kissed by him. She knew how hard the muscles beneath the ill-fitting cotton were. She could see a swirl of dark hair in the deep V-neck of the tunic top. She could almost feel the air being moved as he sucked in a breath. Amy focused on his hand, lying lightly on the high counter in front of the nurses' station. Long, elegant fingers drumming almost imperceptibly to denote, what? Impatience? Tension?

Maybe both, Amy decided, her gaze flicking up to note the faint shadows under his eyes and the way the muscles of his jaw were bunched.

'I called the transplant co-ordination centre first thing this morning,' he told Amy. 'I had to leave a message because it was too early, but they just called me back.'

Amy nodded. She couldn't read whether the news was hopeful or not in his expression. Instead, she got the curious impression that he was watching her just as carefully.

'Summer's at the top of the list.'

'Oh!' Amy caught her breath. And held it, knowing that Luke had something more to say. She could *see* it. Like a tiny flame in the depths of his dark eyes.

A ray of hope.

'There's a child,' Luke said quietly. 'In Scotland. Glasgow's Eastern Infirmary. She's been in a coma for three weeks now and the parents are ready to consider organ donation. The latest EEG showed some activity, however, so she doesn't yet meet the criteria for being a donor, but the activity has declined markedly since the last test. She's showing signs of multi-system failure but they're continuing life support in the hope that some good may come from it. They're going to repeat the EEG later today.'

Amy could feel tears prickling. 'The poor family! What a terrible ordeal for them.'

'Sounds like it might be a release in some ways,' Luke said steadily. 'This girl has severe intellectual and physical disabilities. She had a seizure and knocked her head hard enough to cause this coma.'

'Do you think…?'

'She sounds like an ideal match.' Luke nodded. 'Same blood group. Good size of heart. She's only a couple of years older than Summer. We'll just have to keep our fingers crossed that things come together. She could die from renal failure before her brain gives up. Or they may find the heart is not suitable when it's harvested. You know the kind of things that can get in the way.'

Amy nodded but she was thinking of the child's family. 'It would be so hard, wouldn't it? To have to send your child to Theatre when they were still on life support. Still breathing. If it was my child, I'd just want to hold it…' Amy had to sniff and blink rather hard. 'Sorry.'

Amy didn't need Luke staring at her to know that her emotive response was both unprofessional and unhelpful.

'Don't be,' was all he said, however. 'These situations are emotional for everyone concerned.'

With the possible exception of himself? He seemed perfectly calm. Totally professional. Sympathetic but detached.

One of the unit staff came out of the office.

'Your secretary just called, Mr Harrington. There's someone in your office who'd like to see you if you have a minute to spare.'

Luke glanced at the wall clock. 'Not really. We're due to start again in Theatre in twenty minutes and I need to see the parents.'

'It's your grandmother,' the clerk said.

'Oh…' The flicker of dark brows went up and then down and the frown made him look as though the surprise was not a pleasant one. 'In that case…' Luke gave Amy a somewhat curt nod. 'We'll talk later.'

She was being dismissed. Summer was forgotten for the

moment and there was no chance of an opportunity to present her plan. Or even to tell him that the tyre repair firm that he must have organised had been to deal with his car. It was frustrating enough to make Amy have to resist the impulse to follow Luke from the unit. She wanted time with him. Alone.

She also looked at the clock. If Luke was due in Theatre in twenty minutes and he wanted a few minutes to reassure his patient's parents, he would probably only allow five to ten minutes to talk to his visitor. If she timed it just right, Amy could catch him as he left his office and she could, at least, ask for an appointment to speak to him later.

They needed to talk about the house. He'd said so himself more than once and it hadn't happened yet. They had been sidetracked by those 'other things'.

Amy sat with Summer for a few more minutes. She was still sleeping peacefully. She caught the attention of Summer's nurse.

'If she wakes up, can you tell her I'll be back soon? I've just got a message to run.'

'Sure.'

Unaware of the determined expression on her face, Amy left the unit and headed towards Luke Harrington's office.

'Grandmother!' Luke shut the door of his office behind him. 'This is a surprise!'

'I was in the city for lunch.' Lady Prudence Harrington sat, ramrod straight, in the chair in front of his desk. She tilted her cheek for a customary greeting. 'With Reginald and Lucy Battersby and her brother.'

'At Barkers?' Automatically, Luke bent to brush a kiss to the papery cheek. Reginald's brother-in-law owned a department store that rivalled Harrod's.

'Of course.'

Luke didn't sit down. 'I haven't much time, I'm sorry. I'm due back in Theatre.'

'So I see.' The smile was tolerant. 'It's acceptable, is it? To be seen in public wearing pyjamas?'

'These are scrubs,' Luke said. 'You've seen surgeons on television.'

'I don't watch television. You know that, Luke.'

'Yes.' Luke had to resist looking at his office clock. 'Is something wrong? You never come to the hospital. You're not unwell in any way, are you?'

'Not at all. I'm as fit as a fiddle. As I said, I've just had lunch with the Battersbys and I had to come past on my way home so I got Henry to drop me off at the front door. A nice young woman at Reception told me where I could find your office. I think we need to have a talk, Luke.'

Luke raised an eyebrow. 'But I'm coming to see you to-morrow.'

There was a moment's silence and Luke noticed the way his grandmother was twisting the gloves she had taken off. It gave the impression the old woman was nervous. Surely not.

'Why didn't you tell me, Luke?' Prudence spoke in a very uncharacteristic rush. 'About that house?'

'Oh…' Luke leaned back against his desk, hooking up one leg, his eyes narrowing a little as he focused on his grand-mother. 'Yes. The house. Giovanni Moretti's house.'

Amy's house.

'Reginald tells me it's being used as some kind of orphan-age. That you're planning to demolish it. That you intend evicting these people immediately.'

Luke said nothing.

'That would be wrong, Luke. Especially at Christmastime.

Unless better accommodation can be found, of course. I think I can help. Lucy and I were talking about it and we decided—'

'Grandmother,' Luke interrupted. He kept his voice low. Calm and collected. There was no point in upsetting someone he respected and loved. His only family, in fact. And he had to give her the benefit of the doubt. Lying was dishonourable and it was not something the Harringtons ever did. 'Did my father ever try to find me?' he asked. 'Did he come to the village? To our house, even?'

'What makes you ask such a thing?'

'It's what his niece told me when I went to the house yesterday.'

Prudence went pale. Luke could see what little colour she had fading rapidly, and for a horrible moment he thought he was about to witness his grandmother collapsing.

'You went to the house? You spoke to a…a cousin?'

'Not exactly.' Amy was distantly related in some fashion but it wasn't that close. Not close enough to be any kind of obstacle.

An obstacle to what, precisely?

Luke had to shake the distracting thought away. 'You haven't answered my question.'

The soft, kid gloves were being strangled. 'You have to understand, Luke. It was a terribly difficult time.'

'He did come, didn't he?'

'Twice. The second time he came with a policeman, but he still had no right to trespass. Henry dealt with him.'

Henry. The devoted chauffeur and maintenance man who was married to Elaine, Harrington Manor's housekeeper. A man who would say or do anything his employer requested.

'And the first time? Was that when you told him I was dead?'

It was his grandmother's turn to be silent. To wait for what was clearly coming.

'You told me my father didn't care about me. That I meant nothing to him. That you were the only family I had or needed.'

'No.' Prudence shook her head. She looked suddenly much more than her eighty-seven years. She looked old and so frail Luke felt a twinge of guilt for confronting her. 'I never *said* that.'

'You let me believe it.'

'It was for your own sake. For all our sakes. Can't you see that, Luke?'

She kept using his name and it was starting to sound strangely formal. Cold, even.

Luca…

'It was wrong,' Luke said heavily. 'You denied me my father, but I was too young to remember him or know what I was missing. What was worse was denying a father his son.'

'It was for your own sake,' Prudence repeated. 'He would have taken you away, Luke. To live in poverty in a foreign country. Your education would have been inadequate at best. You wouldn't be the person you are today. I only wanted what was best for you. *You.* My grandson. The only person who is going to carry the Harrington name forward.'

A sensation akin to horror was crawling on Luke's skin. The enormity of what had been done, albeit with the best of intentions. A man's life had been cruelly damaged and— It was true, he might not have become who he was if things had been different.

'Are you not happy with the life you've had, Luke?' His grandmother was rallying now. Gathering her pride as she convinced herself, yet again, that she had done what had been only right and proper. 'You've had the best of everything. You're successful and important. I'm very, very proud of you.'

She was. She was also a strong, proud woman who had been fiercely independent since being widowed when her only child had been young. For the first time Luke had an inkling of how important *he* had been to her. The only link to a beloved husband and daughter. Without him in her life, she would now be a very lonely old woman, living virtually alone in an isolated mausoleum of a family home.

So very, very different to the kind of home and family Luke might have had with his father.

And Amy.

A messy, warm, volatile domestic mix.

Chaos versus order.

Crowds against solitude.

Making do instead of success.

The benefits of what he'd been given were obvious, so why did he feel so confused? Why did he feel the urge to grab his coat from the hook on the door, find that photograph and hold it under his grandmother's nose? He was dangerously close to doing something as unspeakable as shouting at her. Telling her she had done something wicked to both his father and himself.

Something that could never be undone.

And perhaps that was the key. If it couldn't be undone, what was the point in overreacting? And there was never any point in reacting to the extent that emotions overrode rational thinking. Luke pushed himself to his feet.

'I must go. We'll have to discuss this at another time.'

'As you wish.' If Prudence was disappointed in any way, she wasn't about to show it. She put a hand on the arm of her chair and started to rise slowly. With another twinge at how frail she seemed, Luke helped her to her feet. He picked up her handbag and the silver-tipped cane she used and then held open the office door.

'Are you all right? Do you need me to come down with you?'

'I shall manage perfectly well, Luke. As I always do. I believe you're needed elsewhere.'

That was true, but Luke walked as far as the lift with his grandmother. The doors opened as soon as he pushed the button and to his surprise a figure bustled forward. Luke had to catch his grandmother's arm to prevent a collision.

'Oh, I'm sorry!'

'Amy!'

'Oh…' Amy's eyes widened. She looked disconcerted. Then she looked at his companion. Prudence stared back.

'This is my grandmother, Amy. Lady Prudence Harrington. Grandmother, this is Amy Phillips, a nurse on my ward.'

'Indeed.' Prudence inclined her head graciously. 'Delighted to meet you, Miss Phillips.'

Amy smiled. 'You, too,' she said. Her eyes held a question as she looked back at Luke. 'You wouldn't have a minute, would you, Mr Harrington? There's something I really wanted to talk to you about.'

'One minute would definitely be the limit,' Luke said. He kissed his grandmother. 'We'll talk later.'

'Indeed,' Prudence agreed as the lift doors slid shut.

Amy was staring at the doors even after they'd shut, a puzzled frown on her face.

'Walk with me,' Luke invited. 'I really have to be in Theatre. We can talk on the way.'

'OK.' Amy gave a little skip as she caught up. Luke headed for the stairs that would take him to the theatre suite on the top floor. 'I have an idea,' she said a little breathlessly.

'Oh?'

'You're planning to get rid of my house and then sell the land and donate all the money to charity, yes?'

Luke stopped. That *had* been the plan. Funny how it seemed a rather long time ago that he'd made it.

'I know you think it's dreadful.' Amy's words tumbled out. 'Disorganised and messy and that maybe the children would be better off somewhere else, but I can prove that's not true.'

'Oh?' Luke was still trying to remember why it had seemed the best course of action.

'Give me a chance,' Amy begged. 'I can fix things in the house. Tidy everything up. Come and see what it's like when Mamma and Rosa are back and it's more...normal.'

He couldn't miss the flush on her cheeks or the way her gaze slid sideways. Whatever was normal for the Phillips household was hardly likely to seem normal for a Harrington.

'After Christmas?' Amy added hopefully.

Christmas!

Luke turned abruptly. 'Come with me,' he commanded.

He was heading back to his office.

Walking so fast Amy had trouble keeping up. She hadn't presented her plan very well, had she? It had been disconcerting, meeting his grandmother like that.

Prudence Harrington.

The old-fashioned given name was familiar but Amy couldn't locate the memory and it made her feel unfocused.

So did being in Luke's office. Especially when he closed the door behind them.

'There,' he said. 'It's for you.'

'What?' Amy could see a chair and a pair of gloves lying on the floor beside it, but surely he couldn't mean them? She looked up at the framed diplomas on the wall. A bookshelf stacked with glossy medical textbooks arranged according to

height. Piles of journals that were probably filed by exact issue numbers. Plastic models of hearts. Everything in its place.
Tidy and precise.

Apart from the large, battered cardboard carton in the corner, with a frond of tinsel poking through where the flaps had
been closed over the top of the box.

'They were going to throw them out,' Luke was saying just
behind her shoulder. 'I thought…'

He had rescued the old decorations from the ward. He was
giving them to *her*.

For their Christmas tree.

For the children.

Amy turned slowly, to look up at the surgeon. This was the
last thing she would have expected and she could see that it
was out of character. Had he asked somebody for something
that was considered rubbish?

Carried it himself, to his private office?

For *her*?

It was like a flash of lightning. A crack in the veneer of a
man considered remote and unfeeling, and Amy could see
clearly into that crack. She could see the lonely boy Margaret
had told her about. She had met the cool woman, generations
removed, who had raised him. She could see someone who
didn't know what it was like to be really loved.

Cherished.

She wanted to hold him. To cherish him.

But all she could do was smile through her tears. 'Thank you.'

'You're welcome. Please, take them. I really have to go now.'

Except he didn't move.

'Would you…think about what I said? About my plan? I'll
do *anything*…'

He was standing close again. Close enough to kiss her. And

he was staring at her mouth. Looking exactly like he had last night in the park. Like he wanted to kiss her. Like he wanted *her*.

'*Anything?*' His voice was husky.

The silent addition of 'Even *this*?' hung in the air as he bent his head to kiss her.

Oh, Lord, did he think she was offering herself? For the sake of saving her house?

She was offering herself, but not for that reason. Because he needed someone. He needed *her*.

And, yes, she would do anything for him.

Especially this.

Amy closed her eyes and gave herself up to the kiss, but it was a kiss barely begun when it was interrupted by a shocked voice.

'*Luke!*'

He stepped back as if Amy had bitten him. Confused, Amy turned to see his grandmother standing in the doorway of the office.

'I thought you were required in the operating theatre, Luke. Urgently.'

'I am.'

'I must have dropped my gloves. I came back.' Prudence gave Amy a look that made her want to check that her blouse was still buttoned and then sink into the floor and vanish.

And then, before she could finish cringing, she was alone. The gloves had been snatched up and given back to their owner and both Luke and his grandmother had gone.

Amy stood there, bemused. She touched her lips with her tongue and she could still taste Luke.

She looked at the box of decorations and she could still see the crack in that veneer. The glimpse into the soul of the man she loved.

But, most of all, she felt reprimanded. Prudence had informed her, with a single glance, of just how completely unsuitable she was. Unacceptable.

Prudence. More than being careful. More like being surrounded by an impenetrable wall. The woman had no soul.

Where on earth had she heard that?

From Uncle Vanni.

He'd said it. About Caroline's mother. Not to Amy, but she'd overheard and she'd known that she would not like this woman if she ever met her. Anyone that had made Uncle Vanni sound that miserable was not a nice person.

Luke was her grandson.

Harrington was the name he had chosen to use for the rest of his life.

It was getting a lot harder to hang on to the thought that Luke might not have known his father had been alive. That he might, in fact, have simply wished him to be dead.

And maybe that was why he really wanted to get rid of the house. How naïve had she been, thinking that she could offer to tidy it up and make everything all right?

Dazed, Amy eyed the box of decorations. She should leave it behind and pointedly refuse a gift from this man.

But that crumpled, messy box didn't belong in this pristine office any more than she did.

Amy picked it up.

And left.

CHAPTER SEVEN

THOSE brave enough to be out in temperatures well below zero, beneath a sky heavy with snow that wasn't ready to fall, turned their heads to watch the young woman, with long dark hair and an angry expression, stalking through the outskirts of Regent's Park with a large cardboard box in her arms.

Amy was oblivious to the stares.

And, yes, she was angry.

Confused.

Horrified, even.

The strength of the feelings she had for Luke were providing the confusion. How could she feel like this about a man who was prepared to destroy the house his own father had lived in? The only remaining link to the life he had built? To break up the only family Giovanni Moretti had retained and to pose a threat to the children who had become his father's life?

You'd have to really hate someone to be that vengeful.

Had he always hated his father? Why? Had Uncle Vanni known all along that it was hatred he had to get past? Had he stayed in London waiting until Luke was old enough to choose for himself whether he had anything to do with his father? Maybe Uncle Vanni had lived with the hope that something would change for all those years.

Lived with the background misery that he was being denied a relationship with his son. His only child. The thought made Amy angry. Very angry. And maybe Uncle Vanni *had* intended to give Luke his house and another will didn't exist. A final plea for forgiveness? With the largest token he could have presented to tell his son how much it had mattered?

Luke was prepared to take that token and hurl it into oblivion.

How on earth could she have fallen in love with someone capable of doing that?

'Zietta Amy!' The twins had been watching for her return from the drawing-room window and they flung the front door open. 'Is that a present? For *us*?'

'It's for all of you. Where's Zoe? And Robert and Andrew and the girls?'

They were all in the kitchen, which seemed overly warm as she'd come in from the outside. Amy peeled off her coat and draped it over a chair and tried not to think about Luke's coat hanging in exactly the same place. The children gathered to stare, wide-eyed, at the box, except for Robert, who stared at Amy.

'How's Summer doing?' he asked gruffly.

'She's much better. She's getting tired very quickly but she was awake and playing with her doll for a while. She's excited about Christmas.'

'Will she be coming home?' Chantelle asked. 'In time for Christmas?'

Amy had to shake her head. 'I don't think so, honey. She needs to be watched very carefully. We're all hoping she might get a new heart very soon but until then she might have to stay in the hospital.'

'*He's* supposed to fix her,' Robert muttered loudly.

'Who?' Chantelle and Kyra were edging closer to the mysterious box and the twins were climbing on chairs to see what was happening.

'G Squared,' Zoe supplied. 'Amy, I'm making baked beans on toast for tea. Is that OK?'

'Sounds good to me.' Beans were vegetables, weren't they?

'What's G Squared?' Chantelle queried.

'Gru—'

'She means Mr Harrington,' Amy interrupted hurriedly. 'Summer's doctor. Let's do some eggs to go on top of the beans,' she added to Zoe. 'Have we got eggs?'

'I'll have a look.' Zoe moved to the fridge and Monty sat up on his blanket, watching her hopefully.

Chantelle touched the box. 'Is that a puppy in there?'

Amy caught Zoe's gaze as her babysitter emerged from the fridge with a carton of eggs. Zoe grinned. 'You've got a puppy already. You might hurt Monty's feelings if you ask for another one.'

Monty obligingly pricked up his ears on hearing his name and did his best to look as appealing as a giant, scruffy dog could look. Marco and Angelo climbed down from their chairs to go and hug him.

Chantelle sighed philosophically and Robert and Kyra took advantage of everybody's attention being on their new pet to move in and fold back the flaps of the box.

'Oh!' Kyra gasped. *'Look!'*

'What? What?' Monty was forgotten as the younger children crowded close.

Kyra reached out to lift a loop of tinsel. 'It's decorations,' she said reverently. 'For our tree.'

'There's a heap of stuff.' Robert sounded impressed. 'Where's it come from?'

'They're old ones from the hospital.' Amy watched as the first of dozens of coloured balls and stars were lifted from the box. Nobody seemed to notice that the balls were a little dull and that some were chipped. Or that the shiny cardboard stars had bent corners. 'Actually, it was Mr Harrington that rescued them from being thrown out.'

Amy had no idea how difficult it might have been for Luke to find time in his busy schedule to do that but the fact that he had gone out of his way at all was amazing. And the way he had offered them to her with that oddly hopeful expression that begged for acceptance had been what had tipped the balance.

A moment that had been a pinpoint in time but one that Amy would always remember because that had been the moment she had fallen in love with Luke Harrington.

Head-over-heels stuff. A love as big as Africa. Bigger.

It didn't make any difference that it might be inappropriate. Or unwise. It had happened, it was as simple as that.

'Oh!' Chantelle was teetering on the edge of a chair to reach further into the box. 'Kyra! Look what I found!'

'I'll get it.' Kyra's arm was longer. 'You'll fall off in a minute.' She lifted something out of the box.

'It's an angel.' Chantelle's eyes were shining. 'For the top of our tree. Oh…it's just what I *always* wanted.'

He should be here, Amy thought suddenly. Luke should be here to see this. A magic moment. A child's pure joy. He should be seeing it because then he would understand how something so small and ordinary to most people could be so important to someone else.

To see the way the two girls hugged each other and how the older boys gathered up the decorations and led the way to their tree, with the twins babbling happily in Italian, the girls holding hands, Robert leading the way carrying the box, and Andrew keeping pace as his right-hand man. A disparate bunch of siblings, certainly, but right now—and for as long as they could remain living together—they were a family.

Amy was torn between wanting to help the children decorate the tree and needing to help Zoe get a meal on the table. She was saved having to make the choice by the telephone ringing and the relief of being able to connect with the missing members of this family.

'Rosa! How are you?'

'Totally exhausted but I've done it, Amy!'

'What?'

'I've managed to get tickets home. In time for Christmas. Almost.'

'Almost?'

'We fly in on Christmas morning. The plane lands at Heathrow really early…6:30 a.m. You wouldn't believe how difficult it's been and it's cost an absolute fortune. I don't know how much more the credit card will stand but we'll try and get presents for all the kids on our way home.'

'They'll be thrilled to see you. How's Nonna?'

'Getting stroppy. I think the doctors were only too pleased to sign a form to say she's fit to travel. Between her and Mamma, the staff have been pulling their hair out. How's Summer?'

'Holding her own, thank goodness.'

Amy told her sister about the faint possibility of a heart becoming available very soon. Inevitably, Luke's name was mentioned, more than once, but Amy resisted asking the question on the tip of her tongue.

'Where are my boys?' Rosa asked. 'Are they behaving?'

'They're wonderful. They're all decorating the tree in the drawing room right now. I'll get them for you in a tick.'

'What are they decorating the tree with?'

'There was a box of things that weren't needed in the ward. Shiny balls and stars and tinsel. Usual sort of stuff but there's an angel, too, for the top. You should have seen Chantelle's face. She's so happy!'

'I wish I was there. How did you score treasure like that?'

'They're old.'

'Doesn't sound as if the kids mind.'

'No. To tell the truth, Rosa, I didn't even know they were being thrown out. It was Mr Harrington that got them for us.'

'Mr Harrington? Summer's surgeon?'

'Yeah.'

'How amazing! He didn't seem like the kind of guy who'd do something like that when I met him last time Summer was in hospital.'

'No.'

'He must be nicer than he looks.' Rosa laughed. 'Not that there's anything wrong with the way he *looks*, from what I remember.' There was a heartbeat's silence. 'Ah! Is there something going on I should know about?'

Amy couldn't deny it, but she could change the subject and ask the question that was still hovering. The one that might allow a window of hope that she was wrong about Luke.

'Do you remember anything about Uncle Vanni's son?'

'Luca? Not really. He was only three when he was killed and our birthdays were on the same day so I was only three, too. Bit young to remember much.'

'You had the same birthday? I never knew that.'

'That was how they knew each other. Mamma and Caroline were in the hospital together and Luca and I were like twins for a year or two. There's lots of photos some-where.'

There was only one Amy could think of. The one on Uncle Vanni's mirror with that chubby, laughing baby. She carried the cordless phone with her as she walked towards the room on impulse.

'So we weren't actually related to Uncle Vanni?' Why did the prospect of that being true make her feel better?

'No. But we adopted Uncle Vanni when we found him in London. He was so miserable. He needed a family and the rest, as they say, is history.'

Amy was in the room now. In front of the dresser. Staring at the gap at the top left-hand corner where that photograph had been. Remembering that flash of guilt she'd seen on Luke's face when he'd appeared in the kitchen, having been snooping around the house.

'Rosa?'

'*Sì?*'

'Did Uncle Vanni ever talk about Caroline's mother?'

'The Prude? Once. He swore me to secrecy and showed me a scrapbook Caroline had started making for Luca. It had her family history and pictures of the house and all sorts of things. It was like a cross between a photo album and a diary. She wrote in it. Mostly about how happy she was but there was a bit about how sad it would be to never see her mother again.'

'What happened to the scrapbook?'

'I have no idea. It was years and years ago and I'd forgotten all about it. Maybe it's still in the same place.'

'Which was?'

'Tucked under all the stuff in his bottom drawer.'

Amy opened the drawer while Rosa was still talking. 'You know, all Uncle Vanni had wanted for years was to visit the graves and put some flowers on them, but they were both buried in some private cemetery beside the family chapel.

Mamma persuaded him to try again and Dad even went with him in his policeman's uniform, but she wouldn't let them into the house and the butler or whoever he was said they would be prosecuted for trespass if they ever set foot on the property again. How horrible was that?'

'Pretty horrible.' Amy had found the leather-bound scrapbook exactly where Rosa had thought it might be. She carried it back to the kitchen. She had been five when they had moved to London, which made her older sister ten at the time. Luke had been the same age. Maybe Luke couldn't be held responsible for what had been said when he'd been five, but ten had been more than old enough to know about his father. To choose whether to have contact or not.

The hope that she might have been wrong died with a painful quiver.

Maybe Prudence had simply done what her grandson had wanted. It was easy enough to imagine a smaller version of Luke with his privileged life so precisely ordered. Had he been ashamed of the fact that his father was Italian? That he had been merely a vineyard worker? Even as an adult, he'd never come looking. Never given Giovanni a single chance.

Should she tell Rosa that her almost twin wasn't dead after all? That he now owned the house they were coming back to just in time for a Christmas celebration?

No. There would be time enough to say what had to be said later.

And Amy had a few things she wanted to say to Luke first. She also had something she intended to show him. She slipped the scrapbook into her red tote bag.

Six o'clock, but it seemed much later.

From the neon-lit interior of St Elizabeth's, it looked pitch-black outside. Luke could see the Christmas lights decorating the lampposts on the main road beyond the car park. He'd just come from the intensive care unit where baby Liam and his other surgical cases for the day were all doing as well as he could hope for. He'd checked on Summer, as well, and she was stable, but who knew how long that would last? Something could tip the balance at any time and send her into heart failure they had no hope of reversing. Or her heart might simply give up the struggle and stop.

Luke paused momentarily. He should put a call through to the Eastern Infirmary in Glasgow and find out what the results had been of the EEG they'd been planning to repeat on that child in the coma. Checking his answering-machine for a message first would be polite, however, so he changed direction to head for his office before going back up to the theatre suite's changing rooms to get out of his scrubs.

He was almost there. Just outside the on-call bedroom he'd used last night, in fact, when he saw a slight figure turn from his office door and stride towards him.

'There you are!'

Luke halted, taken aback by the anger he could hear in Amy's voice. What had he done? The last contact he'd had with this woman had been in his office earlier that afternoon. Rather close physical contact, and he hadn't been aware of any undercurrent of antagonism at the time.

Far from it!

Had Amy been as embarrassed as he had been when his grandmother had interrupted them? Was that what was upsetting her?

No. The commanding tone of the single word she spoke next put paid to that theory.

'*Luca!*'

He said nothing.

'Why?' Amy asked with deceptive softness. 'Why did you hate him so much? What did your father ever do to deserve that?'

'He was never a father to me.' Luke spoke just as quietly and he glanced swiftly around, but there was nobody to overhear. Nevertheless, this was a conversation that should be private. His office? The on-call room right beside them?

But Amy wasn't going anywhere. She planted her hands on her hips and glared up at him.

'And whose choice was that? You wouldn't let him be a father to you, would you? You refused to see him. Did he know that? Had he had to pretend to his family that you had died so he didn't have to admit to the shame of having a son who didn't want anything to do with him?'

'No! It wasn't like that. It was him who wanted nothing to do with me. Or so I thought. I grew up believing he didn't care.'

'Pfff!' The sound was outraged. 'It very nearly destroyed him, *Luca*!'

He wished she wouldn't say his name like that. He *wasn't* Luca. Hadn't been since before he could remember.

'He loved you. *So* much. As much as he loved your mother.' Amy sucked in a breath. 'Why did you steal the photograph?'

'I…ah…' God, she was mesmerising. Her face alight with the intensity of her emotions. Her eyes flashing sparks of fury.

'You destroyed it, didn't you?'

'No.'

'You're planning to. Just like you're planning to destroy his house.'

Luke couldn't deny it.

'You don't want to believe he loved you. That he would have died for you. That all he ever wanted was a chance to love you.'

'Listen to me,' Luke snarled. He put his hands on Amy's shoulders and turned her so that her back was against the wall. So she would have to look up and listen. 'I never knew he came looking for me. My grandmother thought she was protecting me. She told Giovanni his son had died. I grew up believing he didn't care and...yes, I hated him and that *was* the reason I wanted to get rid of the house, but now...'

'Now?'

'Now I'm not sure. I need time to figure out what to do. What it is I...want...' Luke's words trailed away. He'd got carried away with what he was saying. So carried away he'd actually forgotten it was possible that someone coming along the corridor could overhear and that his most private life could become a subject of gossip. Or observe him with his hands on a female colleague. Leaning towards her, for all the world as though he was about to kiss her.

Worst of all, he didn't give a damn.

Because he knew what he wanted. He was touching it and his hands were burning.

'Luca?' The word was a whisper and Amy's gaze clung to his. Her lips were slightly parted and the flush of anger sill tinged her cheeks. 'What *do* you want?'

Luke reached down beside Amy. To turn the handle of the door and push it open. He turned Amy's shoulder with his other hand and drew her into the privacy of the on-call bedroom.

'You,' he said, his voice raw. 'God help me, Amy. I want *you*.'

* * *

Amy was, quite literally, being swept off her feet.

Into a small room that Luke's presence filled with an overpowering force, even before he closed and locked the door behind them.

An outside window with curtains that were only half-drawn allowed light to filter in from the outside world. Just enough to give form to the force overpowering every one of Amy's other senses.

Not that she really needed to see Luke. She could feel him with every cell of her body. Smell his maleness and his arousal. Breathe him in along with the air she managed to snatch before his lips claimed hers with a hunger that could have been frightening.

Except it wasn't because her own hunger matched his. Her lips were parted before contact was made and her tongue tangled with Luke's before she gave in with a groan of need and allowed his to penetrate her mouth unhindered. The shaft of desire it sparked was so intense she groaned again, helping Luke as he rucked up her skirt, gripped her hips and pulled her against his hardness that the thin cotton of his scrub pants did nothing to restrict.

Thin layers of cotton and silk were the only barriers to the penetration her body was desperate for, and Amy couldn't wait. She slid her hands beneath Luke's tunic top to feel the smooth skin of his back and then her hands moved down and it was so easy to slip them beneath the elastic of the loose pants and delight in taking hold of buttocks that felt like silk-covered steel.

Luke echoed her own sounds of need and Amy's feet left the floor again as she was lifted and placed on the narrow bed. Not that she noticed the size of the bed. Or even the room. Luke filled the space. The room *was* Luke.

Her blouse lost at least one button and her bra was unfastened but not removed. Luke simply pushed it aside as his hands cupped her breasts. Then his lips and tongue replaced the brush of his fingers and Amy cried out softly as she felt the graze of his teeth against nipples that had never been this sensitive.

Clothes were a nuisance, bunched and clinging, but the luxury of getting naked was going to take too much time for either of them so they dragged them aside only as much as absolutely necessary and ignored the discomfort. They were unaware of it in the throes of physical passion, the likes of which Amy had certainly never experienced.

It was crazy. White-hot lust that carried her to the brink of insanity and then exploded. It wasn't until well after Luke had shuddered in her arms in the wake of his own climax and then slowly—heartbeat by heartbeat—relaxed against her that Amy could start thinking again.

Not that she wanted to think of anything other than the sensation of lying in Luke's arms like this. The patches of their skin that were naked still in contact. His breath, ragged against the side of her neck. His hands still holding her as though they never wanted to let her go. Her own arms were around him.

Holding *him*.

An embrace that was so tender it was heart-breaking.

She should say something, but what?

That was amazing?

I never knew sex could be that good?

I love you, Luca?

What would he say to that? That he wasn't Luca, he was Luke? A Harrington? That while the sex had certainly been good, this was a relationship that could never go any further?

Safer to remain silent and not risk hearing something that

could destroy what was still the most magic moment of Amy's life.

One that had, beyond any other, taken her breath away.

In the end, the transformation from Luca to Luke happened rapidly thanks to the strident sound of his pager coming from somewhere on the floor. Amy could feel the way reality came between them, breaking the connection. Making every muscle in Luke's body tense as he reached for the phone on the beside table.

'Harrington.'

He listened for less than a minute. 'I'm on my way,' he said.

He turned back to Amy. 'The EEG on the child in Glasgow was negative. The parents have signed donor-consent forms. Summer's heart's on the way.'

CHAPTER EIGHT

WHAT had he done?

For the next hour, Luke had no time to think about anything other than the logistics of bringing a donor heart to a dying child. Co-ordinating the harvest surgery in Glasgow, the helicopter that would rush it to London and his own part in the procedure—starting the surgery on Summer and getting her onto a heart-lung bypass machine, trimming and preparing the donor heart as soon as it arrived and then removing Summer's heart, matching the excision as exactly as possible to the same shape as the donor organ.

To create a perfect match.

This had to work because it would save Summer's life and...for the first time, Luke's motivation had a new edge. That he was doing this for Amy, as well as Summer, could not be dismissed as irrelevant.

It was a gift that would bring tears of joy to her eyes. An amazing gift that Luke was capable of bestowing, and Amy would love it.

Would she love *him* for giving it?

A respite in organisation came when everything was set up. The surgery would start in Glasgow and a phone line was being kept open, linking the theatres. When the donor heart was removed and pronounced viable, the clock would start ticking in London and Summer would move into Theatre and go under the anaesthetic. She was already in the anteroom and under mild sedation but the small girl did not seem at all frightened.

Why would she be?

She lay cuddled in Amy's arms and Luke knew exactly how that felt. How much was being given. And that was when the enormity of what had happened in the on-call room hit home.

Luke had never been cuddled. His grandmother loved him, he knew that, but she wasn't capable of being physically demonstrative. Maybe she never had been. Maybe that had contributed to his mother falling in love with someone who could show her how important that kind of comfort was. His own parents had certainly been comfortable with close contact. He could tell that from that photograph he had looked at many times since he had stolen it.

So he had known love through touch and then it had been wrenched from his life and he hadn't experienced it again.

Until now.

He wasn't a virgin. Far from it. But he'd never, ever felt threatened by sex.

Afraid.

Afraid he'd found something he'd been looking for his entire life because, having found it, he would have to live with the fear—no, the *knowledge*—that it could be wrenched away from him.

No. His heart told him he could trust Amy. With his life.

He could hear her reassuring Summer.

'Everything's fine, *cara*. It's going to be all right. I'm taking care of you. I'm taking care of everything.'

Everything?

What did that mean?

Oh… Yes…

Luke's brain dredged up what was ringing the alarm bell and his head had always won over anything his heart had to say. Good and bad. That's why he had learned to listen and follow what it said. Rational thinking over emotion. His head had something very different to his heart to say right now.

You can't trust it, it said. *Remember!*

Remember what?

Remember what she said.

What did she say?

She'd do anything to save that damned house. To keep it for her family. Anything! *And she just said it again, didn't she? She's taking care of everything.*

She might have meant the operation. The other children. Christmas.

No. She had sex with you because she wants something.

Me. She wants me the same way I want her.

No. She wants the house. That's all. Remember? She'd do anything!

It was true. He'd looked at her in his office and the desire to hold her and kiss her had been overwhelming, and she'd said she'd do anything and his body had screamed the question—*even this?*

And her eyes had given him the answer. *Yes.* Especially this.

She may have wanted it as much as he had, but had that been because she was prepared to do anything to save her home and he'd just gone along with it? His grandmother had been horrified that he was kissing Amy in his office. How shocked would she be to know he'd had sex with her in the on-call bedroom? Good grief, what if *that* hit the grapevine? His reputation would be ruined. Amy could blackmail him with that if she was so inclined. The thought sent a chill down his spine. He could not allow that to happen.

He could make sure it didn't. She could *have* the damned house. He'd hand it to her on a plate and see if that made a difference. He'd be able to tell. Her face. Those eyes—they were so incredibly expressive. If the house was all she'd wanted, he'd see satisfaction for payment of services rendered. Victory would be written there for him to read.

And if he saw something else?

There was no time to contemplate that scenario.

'The Eastern Infirmary's called through,' a nurse relayed. 'Heart's good. It's being chilled and packed now and the helicopter is standing by on the roof.'

'Code green, then.' Luke simply nodded at the anaesthetist, any personal thoughts banished instantly. 'You start while I'm scrubbing.'

He had to ignore the flash of fear in Amy's eyes. The way she used both her hands to stroke the child's face as she bent down for a final kiss.

'It's all right, *cara*,' she whispered. 'I'll be here when you wake up. Everything's going to be fine.'

The surgery was going to take hours. Rather than wait and pace outside Theatre, Amy chose to go home. While Zoe was happy to babysit and Robert proud to help, they were still both too young to have complete responsibility for the others, especially two lively six-year-old twins.

Part of Amy wanted nothing more than to stay and keep vigil and she was missing her mother and sister more right now than ever, but that was another reason to leave for a while. She needed to call them and tell them about this new, potentially miraculous development in Summer's life.

She would also need to answer the questions and give information that Marcella would demand to know even if she couldn't understand it. Amy rehearsed how she might explain the procedure in simple terms as she hurried home through the icy, dark evening, her mobile phone clutched in her hand in case her friend who worked in Recovery texted her with any news of progress in Theatre 3. Summer's theatre.

She took the time to reassure all the children and admire the newly decorated tree. Chantelle was beaming.

'Robert said we'd keep my paper streamers, as well, 'cos they're really cool.'

The look Robert exchanged with Amy was so full of adult comprehension and caring that she had to give him a hug. He stood there a bit stiffly and didn't return the affectionate gesture, but she could tell he liked it by how gruff his voice was.

'I'll get the twins to bed,' he said. 'Come on, you lot. It's getting late and it's Christmas Eve tomorrow. If you're not good, you won't get presents.'

'We're good,' Angelo insisted, chasing Marco to catch up with Robert. 'Aren't we, Roberto?'

'Sometimes,' he conceded. 'Come on. Scoot!'

The twins scooted. Amy put some fuel onto the drawing-room fire near the tree and tucked the guard securely into place. She patted Monty, who was lying on the hearth rug with Kyra, Chantelle and Andrew, and then she took another moment to admire the tree. She would have to remember to bank the fire again tomorrow night when she tiptoed in with the gifts currently in hiding under Uncle Vanni's bed. With the room warm and the tree looking so festive, Christmas morning was going to be something to look forward to.

Especially if they had good news about Summer to celebrate.

It was more than time to let Summer's official foster-mother know what was going on.

'How do they do it?' Marcella fretted. 'How can they do it in time? What happens when they take the old heart out? Is there just nothing there? An empty chest? *Dio mio*, but what happens to all the blood?'

'There's no blood,' Amy assured her. 'There's a special machine and all the blood goes through that. It gets oxygenated and goes to and from the rest of the body but leaves the heart out of the loop. There's special tubes—like a roadworks diversion.'

'So there *is* just an empty chest? *Oh…* Oh, my poor little angel! How do they do it, Amy? How do they put the new heart in exactly the right place?'

'It's actually quite straightforward,' Amy told her. 'Honestly! It takes ages because they have to stitch everything into place very carefully but it's a matter of joining up all the arteries and veins.'

It was too much information for Marcella. She needed to go and call on every saint she could think of to look after her 'angel'. Rosa wanted to know, however.

'So how do they join them? Like darning them on from the outside?'

'No. They cut the donor heart open and the first thing they do is stitch the pulmonary vein and arteries into place. They're the ones that take blood from the heart to the lungs and then back to the heart again. They have to join in the aorta which is the big vessel that takes blood to the rest of the body, and the big veins that bring the blood back to the heart again.'

'Isn't there a danger of things leaking?'

'The stitches are microscopic—that's why it takes so long. And they use a special glue stuff on the suture lines, as well. It's not likely that there'll be a leak but they have all sorts of special catheters in place afterwards and can measure exact pressures in the heart so they know if there is a problem and it's easy enough to go back in and fix it.'

'Does the new heart just start by itself? When it gets blood inside it?'

'Sometimes.'

'What do they do if it doesn't start by itself?'

'They have a special defibrillator that can be used right on the heart. Tiny little paddles that only give a very small shock.'

'How long will it take?'

'Hours. I'll call or text any news I get.'

'OK. You take care of yourself, too, Amy. Make sure you get some rest. Oh, Mamma wants to talk to you ag—'

The phone seemed to have been wrenched from her sister's hand. 'Amy? Will it work?' Marcella demanded tearfully. 'Will my little *angelo* get through this? I can't believe I'm not there to be beside her bed. To pray for her.'

'I know. I'm sorry, Mamma. I want you to be here, too, but this was a gift that couldn't wait and it might not happen again.'

'Why aren't *you* there?'

'I came home for a bit just to check everything was all right. And it is. Zoe's being a star and you won't believe how much Robert's grown up while you've been away. He really is the man of the house at the moment, Mamma. You'll be so proud of him.'

She could hear Rosa making soothing noises and then her sister took the phone back.

'It's OK, I'll look after her. Are you going back to the hospital now?'

'Very soon. I'll be there for her when she comes out of Theatre.'

'Will she wake up then?'

'No. I think they keep them well sedated for a day or two. On life support. Tell Mamma it's quite possible *she'll* be able to be with Summer when she does wake up.'

It was nearly dawn on Christmas Eve when Summer left the recovery area and was taken back to isolation in the intensive care unit, almost invisible in the midst of the bank of life-support machinery. She was on a ventilator, calibrated bottles hung from her bed for chest and urine drainage and tubes snaked into her skin in various places, allowing administration of drugs and monitoring of her blood pressures and oxygen levels. Electrodes were in place for continuous monitoring of the rhythm of her new heart.

Emergency gear cluttered trolleys. Equipment for suction, dressings, a pacemaker if it was needed and a defibrillator for a worst-case scenario of cardiac arrest. There were people everywhere. Gowned and masked in accordance with isolation protocols that would protect Summer from infection. Her cardiologist and her surgeon and his registrar. The ICU consultant and her registrars. Nurses and technicians.

And Amy, though not for long.

It was overwhelming. Both the level of care Summer would need for the next twenty-four hours or so and the fact that the procedure had been pronounced successful. Textbook perfect, in fact.

Summer had a new heart. It was quite possible she was going to live for a long time. Long enough to experience all the joys life could offer because she would be able to do all the things that normal, healthy children took for granted. To run and play. To go to school. To look forward to her birth-days and Christmases to come.

On top of the anxiety for the period of recovery, gratitude that a donor organ had become available and relief that the surgery had gone so well, Amy hadn't slept for more than twenty-four hours and had only had a restless few hours before that.

And, just to top that off, she had experienced the most emotional, intense love-making she had ever known, because she had been with the man she loved.

And would love, for the rest of her life.

It was all too much and if Amy didn't get home and sleep for a few hours, she would simply collapse. She had already rung Marcella and Rosa and given them the good news. She would tell the other children when they woke up, which hopefully wouldn't be for a little while. If she let Marco and Angelo climb into bed with her for a cuddle, she might get an extra hour's rest.

There would be time after that to thank Luke. It was far too soon to contemplate saying anything more. Hinting about how she felt, for example. She had done that with her body, in any case. Now she had to wait to see if the message was one that would be welcomed.

Until then, she couldn't afford to think any further ahead. She wouldn't begin to worry about the disparity of their back-grounds or the way they viewed life or the huge obstacle Luke's grandmother represented.

Thanking him was enough for now.

For what he'd done for Summer…and for her.

For simply being *him*.

Luke saw Amy leave.

He was deep in conversation with the other consultants,

talking about ventricular function and wedge pressures and when they could start thinking about weaning Summer from the ventilation, but he had sensed Amy's departure.

He tried to catch her gaze, to signal that he wanted to talk to her, but her focus was still on Summer as she slipped from the unit.

Things were well under control here. Luke had done his part and it had all gone extremely well. As close to a perfect procedure as anyone could have wished. Amy knew that. He'd seen the relief on her face when he'd pushed open the doors of the theatre, accompanying Summer to the recovery area, and had paused to tell Amy how happy he was with the way it had gone. He'd seen tears on her cheeks and had had to resist the strongest urge to brush them away himself. He couldn't, of course, not with a dozen colleagues so close and a child that needed intensive monitoring for hours yet.

The chance to share more than those few words hadn't come again but Luke hadn't pushed it. He wanted their next conversation to be private. No distractions, so he could see the effect of what he had to tell her.

That her Christmas gift would be the house. He would instruct Reginald Battersby to do whatever necessary to overrule his father's will and put the house into the ownership of the Phillips family.

He could catch her now, couldn't he? There was nothing more he could do here than watch and wait, to keep in close touch with the consultants now responsible for Summer and to keep himself available in the unlikely event of a complication that needed surgical intervention.

If he hurried, he could catch up with Amy. He'd have to grab his coat, which would look a little odd over his scrubs and white gumboots, but if he ran, he could probably close the distance before Amy reached the park. And how many people would be out and about this early on Christmas Eve?

Way too many people, it seemed. The traffic was heavy and everybody stared at the white gumboots beneath Luke's long, black coat. He hadn't bothered to grab his scarf or gloves and the first flurry of snow was finally starting to fall. His hands were frozen by the time he was striding rapidly though Regent's Park. Just short of running, so he didn't alarm too many people. He stuck his hands in his pockets and he could feel something he'd forgotten for the moment.

The photograph.

He pulled it out as he walked, shaking his head at how uncharacteristic a thing it had been to do—to steal this item.

Except, it was his, wasn't it—from a moral point of view?

The first, and only, inkling he'd had that he had been conceived and born with love. Surrounded by it when he had been too young to remember.

Possibly not too young. Did his soul remember? Was that why it recognised that what he'd found with Amy was so precious?

Something he couldn't afford to lose?

Luke increased his pace, which had unconsciously slowed as he'd looked at the photograph, but he'd been further behind Amy than he'd realised. She was about to leave the park and start down Sullivan Ave. She would be at her house in less than a minute.

The house she didn't know was really going to be hers.

'Amy!'

She turned, saw Luke and stopped dead in her tracks. Took in the white gumboots and the flash of pale blue scrubs that were showing with his coat flapping. He could see the way her face paled and her gloved hand touched her chest over her heart.

She thought he was chasing her to tell her something dreadful. That Summer had died?

'It's all right,' Luke called. 'I just need to talk to you.'

She was still afraid and Luke wanted to take her into his arms. As he closed the distance between them, he became aware of a loud sound behind him. A siren that was coming rapidly closer.

Just as he reached Amy, the fire engine passed them. So close it was automatic to grab Amy and pull her further onto the safety of the footpath. The siren was switched off but the beacons were still flashing. Snow was falling more thickly now and the dense grey white of the sky and snowflakes reflected the bright colours of the beacons, making them seem twice as bright. Twice as urgent.

The huge vehicle had stopped just down the street and another came around the corner, also silencing its siren the way they did when they reached their destination and no longer had to warn traffic to move. Both Luke and Amy watched as firemen in boots and helmets and fire-retardant clothing jumped from the vehicles. Luke let go of Amy's shoulders and somehow her hand slipped into his.

A fire hydrant was being opened and hoses unrolled—all in the space of seconds. Some of the firemen were wearing breathing apparatus, with masks on their faces and oxygen cylinders in packs on their backs.

'Oh, my God,' Amy said. 'Something must actually be on fire.'

They started moving, drawn towards the vehicles, as were other people who had started to gather on the footpath.

'It's close to our house,' Amy noted. A heartbeat later, she gasped. 'It *is* our house! Oh…*Luca!*'

He still had hold of her hand.

They both began to run.

CHAPTER NINE

'STAY out,' a fireman ordered. 'You can't go in there.'

'It's my house,' Amy shouted. 'There are *children* in there!'

'We'll get them out. Stay back!'

There was smoke pouring through a broken window in the drawing room but there was no sign of any flames or smoke from upstairs. A fireman lifted an axe to break open the front door.

'No!' The cry was one of despair. This looked like an execution. Her house was being sacrificed, which wouldn't have mattered a damn if it affected the safety of her children, but it wasn't necessary. 'Don't do that! Please. I've got a key.'

'Hurry up, then.'

Amy fumbled with the key. Luke was right beside her and he took it from her hand, slid it into the lock and pushed the door open.

Heat and smoke billowed out and Amy felt it scorch her throat. Her eyes stung and watered and she started coughing.

'Oi!' Someone sounded furious but she couldn't see through the smoke. Rough hands grabbed her arms and she was pulled backwards and then turned towards where an ambulance was backing towards the scene, its beacons flashing.

Amy craned her neck, blinking. The first rush of smoke

through the front door had lessened and it didn't look nearly as bad as it had. Hoses were being unrolled and carried into her house.

Where was Luke?

'Mad bastard,' she heard someone shout. 'We couldn't stop him.'

Amy's heart did a peculiar kind of somersault. Had Luke gone in there himself? Why? There were firemen here with safety equipment. Luke had to be risking his life to go inside the house. Had instinct overridden common sense? Was he doing it for *her* family?

For *her*?

'What?' Another man was wearing a fluorescent jerkin with the words 'Scene Commander' in bold, black letters. 'Get him out.'

The back doors of the ambulance were flung open. A paramedic urged Amy to climb the steps.

'Let's give you a bit of oxygen,' the young woman said. 'You've inhaled a good dose of smoke.'

But Amy shook her head. She just had an irritated throat, which was making her cough if she tried to take a deep breath. No big deal, and she wasn't going anywhere she couldn't see her front door. She didn't need to breathe deeply at the moment. She couldn't. Not until she saw everyone she loved coming out of that door safely.

Including Luca.

Especially Luca.

The first figures came through the smoke and then into the now thickly swirling snow. Bare feet and pyjamas. Robert was holding Kyra's hand and right behind him came a fireman with a twin under each arm. Marco and Angelo were shrieking with fright.

They all came towards Amy. A second ambulance was pulling up and there seemed to be people everywhere, holding blankets and oxygen cylinders.

'*Zietta*…Amy…' Marco was coughing and sobbing, holding his arms out.

'*Mi*! Me, too!' Angelo made an identical picture and already the distressed boys were shivering uncontrollably.

Amy found herself sitting on the back steps of the ambulance with a child clinging on each side. Blankets were wrapped over them all and paramedics fussed with oxygen masks and stethoscopes.

Robert was right beside the steps, refusing to climb into the second ambulance. Kyra was clinging to him, sharing his bright red woollen blanket, and they both needed to be close to Amy.

There was still no sign of Luke. Or Zoe or Andrew or Chantelle. Amy's heart pounded and then stopped for a beat as a new figure emerged. Another fireman, with Andrew in his arms. Andrew was also crying and held his arms out to Amy. Robert and Kyra wriggled closer and her view of the front door was completely obscured.

'Robert?' Amy tried to disentangle herself. 'Can you sit here? I need to find Chantelle and Zoe.'

And Luke.

'*No!*' the twins wailed. 'Don't go away, Zietta Amy!'

'I'll be right back,' Amy promised. 'You're safe now. Be brave for just a minute or two. Can you do that for me, darlings?'

Robert towered over the younger children. 'We can do that.' He coughed harshly. 'Can't we, guys?'

A chorus of assents, coughs and stifled sobs was what Amy left as she ran towards the people now coming out of the house.

Four people. Two firemen. One was carrying Chantelle and the other had his arm supporting Zoe. He peeled his mask from his face.

'The kid had locked herself in the bathroom,' he said. 'That bloke got her out.'

'She was...too scared...to open it.' Zoe had runnels of black eyeliner on her cheeks and looked a lot younger than her sixteen years. 'Amy...I'm so sorry.'

'It's not your fault,' Amy said firmly. 'And you're all safe, that's all that matters.'

Except they weren't all safe, were they?

Where was Luke?

The fireman was obviously thinking the same thing. He looked over his shoulder. 'He was supposed to follow us out. Where the hell has he gone now?'

Amy helped guide Chantelle towards the others. The twins had been persuaded to get into the shelter of the ambulance and they were both cocooned in red blankets. Wide-eyed, they stared out at the scene.

'Firemen!' Marco said, awed. 'And policemen!'

'And doctors,' Angelo added, looking at the uniform of the paramedic.

'There's flames,' Chantelle sobbed. 'Our Christmas tree is burning up.'

Could that have been what had caused the fire? All those paper streamers and an open fire not that far away and a rogue draft, maybe? But Amy had checked the fire carefully. The guard had been in place. The children all knew how important it was to be careful not to knock the guard.

Self-recrimination hovered but the extent of the damage was an unknown.

Nothing material mattered, anyway.

Where was Luke?

'*Where* is he?' Amy shouted at the scene commander. 'You have to find Luke. Mr Harrington. The man who went in first….'

'We'll find him. Go back to your children, lady. They need you.'

So does Luca, Amy thought desperately.

'For God's sake,' the man beside her growled. 'He risked his damn life for a *mutt*?'

'What?' Amy whirled back to face the house and there was Luke, stumbling a little with a fireman on either side of him, his arms full of a large, limp-looking dog.

'Monty!' Amy had completely forgotten about the newest member of their family. Luke's face was blackened by smoke and she could hear the harsh rasp of his breathing as he came closer.

'Monty!' Children poured from the back of both ambulances and crowded around as Luke laid the dog down gently.

Zoe was crying again. 'Is he dead?'

Luke shook his head. 'Too…much…smoke.'

'Same for you, mate. Here.' A paramedic slipped an oxygen mask over Luke's face.

'Monty needs one, too.' Robert's voice was deep. It had a new edge to it that Amy hadn't heard before. A commanding edge. The teenager eyed the paramedics' raised eyebrows. 'He's not just a dog, OK? He's one of us now.'

Luke had taken as deep a breath of the oxygen as he could. He coughed, took another breath and then slipped his mask off. He held it over Monty's huge black nose.

'Hey!' The paramedic sounded concerned. 'You need that more than the dog.'

But Luke shook his head and the paramedic shrugged. 'Guess I'll find another cylinder, then.'

'And a blanket?' Chantelle pleaded. 'It's awfully cold out here.'

A minute or two later the children were red blobs crouched beside Monty, who was also covered in a red blanket. Luke's breathing sounded almost normal again and to everyone's intense relief Monty was recovering. He tried to get up but Marco and Angelo were hugging him too tightly so he gave up and thumped his tail a couple of times instead.

'Thank goodness,' breathed Amy. She turned to thank Luke for saving the dog, but he was standing beside the scene commander.

'The kitchen seem's fine,' he was saying. 'A lot of smoke but nothing was burning. The dog was still trying to bark and warn everybody but he'd lost his voice and then he got another lungful of smoke and collapsed.'

There were people all around. The numbers and levels of activity had been steadily increasing but Amy hadn't noticed because she had been standing with an arm around both Chantelle and Kyra, watching for any sign of Monty's recovery.

'Fire's out!' A fireman was reporting to the scene commander now. 'Started in the main room, by the look of things, with a Christmas tree by the fire.'

'Is the house structurally damaged?' Luke asked.

'It will need to be properly assessed and that isn't likely to happen today. It's uninhabitable for the moment, that's for sure. Smoke and water creates one hell of a mess.'

'What about the occupants?'

He sounded so clinical, Amy thought with dismay. 'The occupants'? She was the woman he'd made love to so recently and these were all children that had already had more than their fair share of heartbreak in their lives.

'The police will deal with that side of things,' the scene commander told Luke. 'And Social Services. You don't need to worry about it.'

Paramedics were trying to herd Amy and the children back to the ambulances.

'We're taking you all to the hospital,' they said. 'You'll all need proper check-ups.'

Amy could hear Luke's pager sounding and saw him flip open his mobile phone. The thought that he might be being summoned because of some complication with Summer added a new level of anxiety. She broke away from the children and hurried towards Luke. Only days ago she wouldn't have dreamed of interrupting a telephone conversation he was having, but things had changed.

'Is that about Summer?'

He gave his head a curt shake. 'I'll be there as soon as I can. I'm five minutes away.' He snapped the phone shut.

'Is Summer all right?' Amy asked. 'I need to get back to her but I'll have to go with the others. They're taking them to hospital, hopefully Lizzie's, seeing as it's the closest, but—'

But Luke was looking down at himself rather than at Amy. The white gumboots were black and the scrub pants wet and filthy from the knees down. 'I'll have to get changed,' Luke said. 'I can't appear in ICU and talk to Liam's parents looking like this, can I?'

'Miss Phillips?' A policeman approached them. 'Can I talk to you, please? We need names and details for all the children involved here. And does this belong to you?'

It was Amy's red tote bag that she must have dropped ages ago when they had been running towards the house.

'Yes, it's mine.' She almost didn't want to claim it, knowing that her cellphone was in there. And that she was going to have to call her mother and tell her about this disaster.

'I have to go,' Luke said.

'Please…check on Summer? I'll be there as soon as I can.' Amy was being torn in too many directions and she was close to tears. She wanted to be with the children. To be with Summer.

To be with Luke.

'Of course,' he said.

'And…and thank you.'

'No need. Anyone would have done what I did.'

No, Amy thought, watching him stride away, dismissing a paramedic's renewed attention with a wave of his hand to indicate he needed no further attention. Not everyone would risk themselves to save other people's children, let alone their dog.

Even fewer people would brush off the chance to be seen as a hero. Or to get involved with the people that had been rescued.

Maybe Luke didn't want to be involved. With any of them.

Amy turned to look at the house. Her home. The front door stood open, snow swirling in to land in puddles in the hallway. Windows were blackened and broken and the reek of hot timber and sodden ash was everywhere. A policeman was putting tape across the gate to forbid entry.

She and the children were now officially homeless. Their clothing, toys and Christmas presents were being closed off from being claimed. Maybe those gifts had been destroyed. They were under Uncle Vanni's bed and his room was right beside the drawing room where the fire had started.

The engines of the ambulances were running and they were about to all be taken away. Amy would have to start answering questions about the children. Who they were and why they were in the house and why the level of supervision had clearly been inadequate.

Another child who needed her lay in the intensive care unit, fighting for her life, and the only other adult members of her family were still twenty-four hours away.

Amy had never felt more alone.

Luke had vanished through the crowd of onlookers, presumably intent on getting back to Lizzie's and his work as soon as possible. He hadn't looked as though he would have preferred to stay and help.

He had looked almost relieved.

And why not? He had got what he'd wanted all along, hadn't he?

The house was, at least partially, destroyed. The authorities were going to make sure that Amy and children couldn't return in the near future. It was possible that even minor structural damage from the fire would be enough to tip the balance and have the house condemned.

With dawning horror, Amy took in the implications.

It was the day before Christmas and she and her family were homeless.

CHAPTER TEN

'SO WHERE are you going to go? Have you got family in London?'

Amy tried to smile at the young constable because he was only trying to be helpful, but her ability to smile seemed to have deserted her. It just made her lips wobble.

'No,' she said. 'My mother and sister are in Italy until tomorrow. My only other family is my grandmother and they're bringing her back with them.'

'We'll have to get Social Services to organise placement for all the children, then.'

'No. Please, don't do that. We need to be together for Christmas. Isn't there any way at all we could go back to our house? If we stayed out of the damaged rooms?'

'You'll be shocked when you see how much damage gets done by thousands of gallons of water being sprayed everywhere. The place is saturated and the electricity and gas are shut off. There'll be no way of heating it and you'd all freeze.'

'What about getting our clothes? Christmas presents?'

'They're probably all wet. Stinking of smoke, anyway. Look, I'm really sorry but there's no way any of you will be going back to that house for the next few days.'

Maybe never, his expression said.

'So you've all got to go somewhere. You can't stay here.'

They couldn't. They'd already been in the emergency department of St Elizabeth's for hours. The children had all been given thorough physical check-ups. They'd been given lunch. They were all in clean, dry hospital pyjamas and still had the red ambulance blankets for extra warmth. Having been allocated a relatives' waiting room and provided with toys, books and DVDs, they had also been visited by Claire—a kind, middle-aged woman from Social Services.

Claire came into the office where Amy was talking to the police constable.

'They're all happy,' she told Amy. 'Except that Zoe wasn't too pleased at being collected by her mother. They wanted to know how Monty was getting on so I rang the vet. He's fine.'

'Oh, that's good news!'

'The clinic's not far from here and he can be collected any time. The children are also asking if they can visit Summer.'

'Not today.' Amy shook her head. She had been able to spend some time in the intensive care unit herself while the children were being assessed, and while Summer was doing brilliantly, she was still sedated and on a ventilator. It would be distressing for the other children to see her like that. Amy had wanted to find out when the life support would be deemed unnecessary but the ICU consultants were busy with a new arrival and Summer's surgeon had been nowhere to be seen.

'Did you get through to your mother and sister?'

Amy nodded this time. That conversation had been dreadful. Rosa had panicked about her sons and Marcella had cried with despair.

'Did they have any ideas about where you can all stay for a few days?'

Inspiration struck Amy. 'We'll go to a hotel,' she said.

'Can you afford that?'

'Yes.' It was a bill that wouldn't need to be paid until they left, wasn't it? Surely the house was insured.

'Have you checked availability? It's not a good time of year to be looking for last-minute accommodation. We do have foster-parents available.'

'We need to stay together,' Amy said stubbornly. 'We'll manage.'

'What about clothes? You'll need to go shopping. You'll need help with babysitting. There's meals to consider.' Claire was looking more and more doubtful. She also looked as though she was gearing herself up to do her duty, however un-pleasant the repercussions might be.

'I know these children will be very upset if they're separ-ated,' she began, 'but I really can't see any way around this.'

The office door opened as she spoke. Luke was back in his pinstriped suit. An authoritative figure that managed to take control before uttering a word.

'I need to talk to Amy for a moment. Excuse us, please.'

She looked dreadful.

As though this was the end of the world.

And, in a way, it was.

In an astonishingly short space of time Amy's world had disintegrated. Because of one family crisis, she had been left responsible for her home and the welfare of a large group of children. Now her home was damaged, possibly beyond repair, one of those children was critically ill and the others were in danger of being split up and having to spend Christmas in a foreign environment, away from anyone who knew and loved them.

Amy looked pale and worried but there was no air of being defeated, and Luke found that immensely admirable. There was no suggestion of accusation in her face, either, but Luke couldn't help a twinge of guilt, even though it had been purely coincidence that the disintegration of Amy's world had accelerated from the moment he had stepped into her life.

He had already decided not to evict the family prior to Christmas. At all, in fact. Not that he'd been able to tell Amy of his decision to hand over the house. It had hardly been the time when they'd seen that the house in question was on fire and the lives of its inhabitants in danger. And there hadn't been a chance since.

The system had enclosed them all. Luke had been juggling his patient commitments, monitoring Summer's condition and had had interviews with both the police and that woman from Social Services.

She had asked how much he knew about the Phillips family.

'Just how well are these children being cared for?'

'They have everything they need,' he had responded. 'Things are difficult at present with Amy's mother being away and the house might not be in perfect condition but these children are warm and well fed and…they're loved.'

'They do seem happy,' Claire had mused. 'And very close to each other. That oldest boy, Robert, is determined that they're going to stay together.'

'Have you spoken to Amy yet?'

'Not properly. I'll do that soon, when I've had a chance to decide what we need to do.'

Luke looked at the way Amy was standing tall in front of him now, her chin raised and determination lurking in anxious eyes, and he knew Claire would find her even more determined than Robert to keep the family together.

It reminded him of their first encounter. Had it really been only two days ago that she'd tried to shut the door in his face? She had demonstrated how fiercely she was prepared to fight for her family.

She'd do anything, she'd said.

Anything.

The word had been echoing in the back of Luke's mind with increasing intensity. His notion of gifting her the house and judging by her reaction whether her love-making had been as genuine as it had seemed was pointless now. The house was damaged and uninhabitable. Such a gift might even be seen as insulting.

So, amongst all the other duties that had kept him running, physically and mentally, for the last few hours, Luke had decided on another approach.

One that was out of character enough to be making him nervous.

Very nervous.

Not only was he going to listen to his heart properly for the first time in his life, he was going to act on what it told him even if it went against what was obviously more rational.

At least, he would, depending on the answer Amy provided to the question he was about to ask.

'You said you'd do anything to save your house, didn't you?'

'Yes.' Amy's smile was wry. 'It's a bit late now to put my plan into action, though, isn't it?'

It wasn't too late for *his* plan, though.

'When you said "anything"?' he asked softly. 'Did that include what happened last night?'

The play of emotions on Amy's face was so clear Luke could actually feel the emotions they represented. Her first reaction was confusion. What had happened last night of such significance? A frown of anxiety appeared. Summer's transplant? No. Amy couldn't see the connection between Summer's surgery and the house. What else had happened?

Amy's expression softened. Her eyes darkened and her lips parted and Luke could see—*feel*—the memory of their time together. A time that had no connection to anything else because it had been simply theirs.

That it had been difficult for Amy to make a connection was all the answer Luke really needed.

But, '*No,*' Amy whispered. 'No, no, no!'

Luke drew in a careful breath. 'Are you still prepared to do anything? To keep the children together and safe for Christmas?'

'Of course.' Amy looked puzzled now. Her gaze was fixed on him. She didn't understand. Their immediate future was about to be dictated by social authorities who had more clout than Luke did in such matters. How could he be in any position to suggest an alternative?

'What do you want me to do?'

Luke's smile was crooked. 'Trust me.'

It was the strangest meeting Amy had ever attended and it was just as well that input from her didn't appear to be required.

Dazed by the events and emotional turmoil of the last few days, she sat on a couch in the relatives' waiting room with the twins on her lap, a girl cuddled close on each side and two older boys flanking the arms of the couch like sentries, watching and listening while Claire asked the questions she should have asked Luke herself.

'What arrangements? What on earth are you planning to do with six children?'

'It's all in hand,' was all Luke seemed prepared to say. 'I'm taking full responsibility for this family.'

'Who did you say you were again?'

'Luke Harrington. Head of the cardiothoracic surgical department here at St Elizabeth's.'

'No.' Claire sounded faintly bewildered. 'That other name you said.'

'On my birth certificate? Luca Moretti.'

The way he said the name sent a curl of something very poignant through Amy. Had he noticed he'd said it with an Italian accent?

He'd been lost for a very long time, this man, and the thought made her heart squeeze tightly.

She loved him.

She trusted him.

More than Claire did, it seemed.

'I still don't understand. It all seems terribly complicated and rather irregular.'

'Let me make it easy for you.' The soothing note in Luke's voice had probably calmed many anxious parents in the past. 'My father—sadly deceased—owned the house Amy and the children live in. I inherited it. Because of that, I'm taking full responsibility for the inhabitants of that house.'

Was that the only reason he wanted to help? Some kind of guilt trip? Amy bit her lip to drive back weary tears and she cuddled the twins closer.

She trusted him. She needed to hang on to that.

Marco obligingly twisted in his half of her lap and wound his arms around her neck. 'I love you, Zietta Amy.'

'I love you, too,' she whispered back.

Luke was speaking more forcefully now. He was not about to allow a social worker to disrupt arrangements he had made. Whatever they were.

'I'll sign whatever forms are necessary. It's getting late and it's Christmas Eve. I'm sure we've both got better things to do than stand here debating this issue.'

Claire glanced at her watch and gave in with a sigh. 'Very well. But I must insist on knowing where you intend taking these children.'

Luke didn't look at Amy to seek her approval.

'Harrington Manor,' was all he said. 'In Harrington village. About an hour's drive from London.'

Claire made a final attempt at regaining some form of control. 'Amy? How do you feel about all this? Are you happy to go with Mr Harrington?'

The thought of being taken so far away from Summer was more than a worry. It was unacceptable. The thought of being in the same house as the old woman who had looked at Amy as though she wasn't fit to scrub her floors almost made her gasp with incredulity. It was impossible!

But small arms were tightening around her neck and the children were all staring at her. Questioning this new turn in their lives. Ready to stand by her and refuse to co-operate if she didn't think it was a good idea. Trusting her to keep them safe.

Amy stared at Luke. She had no choice here. She *had* to trust him.

He met her gaze without smiling and his eyes reiterated the words he had spoken in the corridor.

Trust me.

Amy turned back to Claire. 'Yes,' she said calmly. 'I'm happy. We'll all go to Harrington Manor.'

One step at a time, she reminded herself. All she could do

was to keep things together as much as possible for as long as possible.

And hope for a miracle.

It took two taxis to ferry them all to Harrington Manor.

Luke followed in his own car.

'I'll need to come back,' he explained as Amy prepared to climb into the first taxi where the twins and Chantelle were waiting. 'Summer's due to have her drains removed and we're thinking of lightening her sedation. She may be ready to come off the ventilator.'

Which meant she could wake up. Soon.

'I need to be there,' Amy said, 'when she wakes up.'

Luke nodded. 'You'll be able to come back. A car and chauffeur will be available. I thought you'd want to go with the children initially.'

A chauffeur? Not Luke? Why was he coming back with them now, then?

Did his grandmother not know they were coming? About to descend en masse on a home that both Uncle Vanni and her father had been threatened with prosecution for trespass if they tried to enter?

Oh…*Lord*!

Snow was falling more thickly and daylight was virtually gone by the time the small entourage finally escaped the city limits. Luke's car had taken some time to catch up with the taxis but the three vehicles were together as they left the motorway and turned onto more rural roads.

'Are we lost?' Chantelle asked.

'No way, darling.' The driver of the black cab was enjoying what would probably turn out to be his biggest fare ever. 'I've got GPS in this baby. No way we can get lost.'

'What's GPS?'

'It means we're being tracked from up in space,' Amy tried to explain. 'That little screen on the dashboard is telling our driver exactly where we are and where we need to go.'

'Space?' Marco sounded puzzled.

'*Spaziale*. Where the stars are.'

The children peered from the windows of the taxi but all they could see was the swirl of snowflakes in the headlights of the small line of cars.

'Will Father Christmas find us when it's snowing?' Chantelle asked. 'How will he know where we've gone?'

'Maybe he's got GPS these days, too.' The cab driver chuckled. Then he glanced in his rear-view mirror and saw the expression on the little girl's face. 'Hey, Santa comes from a very snowy place. It's no problem.'

Amy had something new to worry about now. The few presents tucked away for the children were lost. Shops might be open until late tonight but with the time it would take to travel back to the city and the time she needed to spend with Summer, how could she manage to fit any shopping in? How on earth could she do anything about giving these children any kind of Christmas surprises?

Would Luke's grandmother even have a tree?

The prospect began to appear unlikely. Huge iron gates swung open a short time later, presumably because Luke had a remote control in his car. Snow was piling up in drifts on either side of the long driveway and it was settling onto bare branches of the massive old trees that gave the impression of a guard of honour.

The house was enormous and dark and forbidding. Even Amy's taxi driver fell silent as they parked at the base of semi-circular stone steps that had huge lions on pillars at each side.

Luke got out of his car and came to Amy's taxi.

'Stay here for just a minute or two,' he instructed. 'I'll be back.'

Amy cuddled the children close and tried to banish her sense of foreboding as the heavy front door opened and the house swallowed Luke.

If Luke had thought his grandmother nervous in his office yesterday, he had to consider her alarmed now. She was standing near the huge fire in the library. Beside a small table with spindly legs on which a decanter of sherry and small crystal glasses stood on a silver tray.

'Whatever's going on, Luke? What are all those taxis doing outside?'

'We have visitors.'

The housekeeper, Elaine, closely followed by her husband Henry, hurried through the door.

'Is everything all right, Lady Harrington?'

'That's what I'm trying to find out myself. Luke?'

'We have visitors, Grandmother. For Christmas.'

'I beg your pardon?'

'Henry said they look like children,' Elaine reported. 'He was watching from the garages.'

Henry looked at his feet. Luke looked at his grandmother just as steadily. 'They are children,' he said. 'There are six of them and they range in age from about six to fourteen.'

'Oh, *my*!' Elaine breathed.

'Are these the children I was trying to discuss with you yesterday, Luke? If so, I can make arrangements. They don't even need to get out of the cabs. Let me call Lucy and—'

'No. I will not allow that.'

His grandmother fluttered a hand, looking shocked.

'There was a fire this morning,' Luke continued. 'The house that is home to these children was extensively damaged. I have brought them here for a reason.'

Prudence sank onto the edge of an overstuffed couch. 'I don't understand.'

'Elaine?' Luke smiled at the housekeeper. 'Could you prepare some rooms, please? At least four, I would think.'

'But…' Elaine looked at her employer, but Prudence had closed her eyes. 'They're *children*…' The word was slightly awed.

'You're good with children, Elaine. Maybe you've still got that box of toys somewhere. You know, the ones they used to keep in the kitchens for me?'

A smile tugged at Elaine's mouth. 'I think I know where it is. Oh, my! Children. Here for Christmas.' She turned away. 'Henry? I'm going to need your help. Let's sort out some linen.'

Prudence opened her eyes and waited. Luke sat on the edge of the couch beside her.

'I know this is a shock,' he began. 'But things have happened in the last couple of days that have made me start to question my life.'

'This has something to do with that nurse, doesn't it? The one you were…ah…'

'Kissing,' Luke supplied. 'Her name is Amy and, yes, it has a lot to do with her, but that's beside the point just now. Look.' He fished in the his coat pocket and brought out a rather crumpled photograph. 'Look at this.'

'Oh!' Prudence put a hand to her throat and tears sprang instantly to her eyes. 'Caroline!'

'She was happy,' Luke said quietly. 'She loved my father and, by all accounts, he adored her. Maybe he wasn't suitable but my mother's death broke his heart. Losing his son was an-other tragedy as far as he was concerned and it was one that he didn't have to suffer.'

Prudence was silent.

'He *did* suffer,' Luke went on. 'And if I don't help his fam-ily and the children he loved, *they* will suffer, and that would be wrong.'

He picked up his grandmother's hand and held it. 'You are my family,' he said, 'and I haven't said this for far too many years but I love you. You did what you thought was right but you took something away from me. The chance to know my father. It's something that I think mattered a great deal.'

'I'm…sorry, Luke. I—'

'I know.' Luke leaned over to kiss her cheek. 'I'm going to bring the children in now. They're frightened and cold and hungry. Please, welcome them because this is also something that matters a great deal.' He stood up. 'We can't turn the clock back but we've got a chance here to do something right. Something honourable. Do it for me. Please?'

'I'll…try.' Prudence took a shaky breath and sat up a little straighter. 'Just for Christmas?'

'Just for Christmas,' Luke agreed.

One step at a time, he told himself as he went back to the waiting cars. For himself, as well, because he was stepping into alien territory here. An emotional landscape that had no map.

They trooped inside, silently.

They stood, silently, gazing at the biggest Christmas tree Amy had ever seen, positioned at the base of a stairway that curled gracefully up and then divided to form a U that swept past an uncountable number of doors.

A woman with grey hair in a bun, holding a pile of linen, beamed down at them before hurrying through one of the doors.

The tree was doing its best to reach the banisters of the U so it had to be at least twenty feet tall, and it was covered with thousands of white fairy lights in the form of tiny icicles that were twinkling on and off in sequence. A discreet few, gorgeously wrapped silver parcels lay at its base.

Luke ushered them on. 'Come into the library,' he commanded. 'My grandmother is waiting to meet you.'

Amy's misgivings made her heart thump alarmingly rapidly but she stepped forward, a twin attached to each hand. Robert, Kyra and Andrew were behind them but Chantelle, her face shining, skipped ahead. She came to an abrupt halt on entering the library, however, because standing in front of a roaring fire, with a forbiddingly remote expression on her face, was the woman who had dismissed Amy yesterday with no more than a passing glance.

Chantelle's mouth dropped open.

'Are you the *queen*?'

For a moment there was an odd silence and Chantelle gave Amy a look of trepidation.

'She *looks* like the queen,' she said in a small voice.

'*Che?*' Marco didn't understand.

'This is my grandmother,' Luke told the children. 'My *nonna*,' he added to Marco and Angelo. He smiled at Chantelle. 'But she does look a bit like the queen, doesn't she?'

Lady Prudence Harrington wasn't smiling but the tension in the room eased just a little. Amy kept her gaze on Luke, loving him so much for the way he hadn't let Chantelle feel she had said something stupid.

'Excuse me for a moment,' Luke said. He vanished through the door and the awkward silence fell again as Prudence stared at the wall of silent children.

'I forgot,' Luke announced as he came back through the door. 'He was asleep on the back seat of my car.'

'Monty!' the twins shrieked in delight.

'Luke!' The tone was as shocked as it had been yesterday when Prudence had caught her grandson kissing a nurse in his office. 'What in heaven's name are you thinking of, bringing a *dog* in here?'

'It's Monty.' Chantelle had been gazing at Lady Harrington as though still convinced she was in the presence of royalty. 'He's *our* dog now.'

'Dogs belong outside.' Prudence moved to push a button on the wall. 'I'm sorry, Luke, but this is too much. I need to call Henry.'

'Come with me.' Luke offered his grandmother his arm. 'We'll both talk to him. And Elaine. We need some hot food and drink for our visitors.'

They were left alone in the library for what seemed a very long time. Amy heard muted voices and more than one door closing. A telephone rang, the fire crackled and a grandfather clock at one end of a huge bookshelf ticked solemnly.

Then a man they hadn't seen before came in.

'I'm Henry,' he told them. 'I have a message for you, Miss Phillips. From Mr Harrington.'

'Call me Amy, please.'

Henry blinked. 'I'm not sure that's—'

'Spit it out, Henry.' The woman with the grey bun came bustling in. 'I'm Elaine,' she told Amy. 'The housekeeper. I've got your rooms ready if you'd like to come and see where you're all going to sleep?'

The children eyed her suspiciously.

'And then we'll all go down to the kitchens,' she added. 'Beryl is making dinner for you. And for— Oh, my! He's a big dog, isn't he?'

'That's Monty,' Chantelle said.

'Well, we'll find some dinner for Monty, too. And some nice old blankets. He could sleep in the scullery where it's all nice and warm from the coal range. If that's suitable?'

Robert gave a slow nod. He approved of Elaine. Amy could feel herself relaxing a little.

'What was the message?' she asked Henry.

'Oh, yes. Mr Harrington had to return to the hospital somewhat urgently. He said you'd be wanting to follow him and I'm at your disposal.'

'You've got another wee one who's sick at the moment, haven't you?' Elaine's face was creased with sympathy. 'Let me settle the others and get them fed and bathed and into bed.'

'That's too much work for you,' Amy protested. 'I'll stay and help.'

Elaine shook her head. 'It's been too long since this house heard the sound of children's voices. It'll be a treat.'

Amy was quite sure Lady Harrington didn't see it as a treat. It seemed rather pointed that she hadn't returned to the library.

Elaine seemed to be reading her thoughts. 'Lady Harrington sends her apologies,' she said, 'but she's not feeling very well and has had to retire to her room. She'll see you in the morning.'

Christmas morning.

'Whenever you're ready, miss,' Henry said kindly. 'And you're not to worry about your family that's coming, either. I'm to stay in the city tonight and meet them at the airport to-morrow. Mr Harrington said to tell you not to worry about anything.' Henry smiled. 'That everything's in hand.'

Things may have been taken out of her own hands but Amy felt curiously safe with the astonishing flow that was pulling them all along. It was as though someone was waving a wand to take care of everything that was worrying her.

A tiny seed of something as effervescent as excitement took hold inside her.

Miracles did happen sometimes, didn't they?

And what better time for a bit of magic than Christmas?

CHAPTER ELEVEN

SHE was asleep.

Tangled, dark hair framed a pale face that was cradled on one arm. The other arm still lay on the bed, fingers cupped around a much smaller hand.

Luke kept his voice low. 'How long has she been asleep?'

'Most of the night. She's woken every time I've done Summer's recordings but she's barely moved.'

Luke gave the latest set of recordings another satisfied glance. Then he turned his head to nod at someone else.

Henry ushered three women into the ICU, his fingers on his lips to warn them of the need to stay quiet and calm, and then he faded back into the corridor. One of the women was easily as old as Luke's grandmother. A small, slightly hunched figure leaning heavily on a walking stick and probably hampered by the long, black skirt she was wearing. The other two looked remarkably like Amy and Luke gave them a smile that came from the bottom of his heart.

'Only a few minutes,' he warned the new arrivals. 'There's only supposed to be one or two close relatives at a time.'

Amy's grandmother scowled at Luke rather ferociously but her mother was clearly struggling with tears. Hyperventilating as she tried to control herself. Luke put both his hands on her shoulders and gave them a reassuring squeeze.

'Summer's doing very, very well, Mrs Phillips. Be strong.' He smiled again. 'I wouldn't be at all surprised if she wakes up when she hears your voice.'

Amy woke up at the sound of her mother's voice. She lurched to her feet to be enveloped in a hug, first from Marcella and then a long, tight, relieved embrace from her older sister.

'*Buon Natale, cara! Buon Natale!*'

'You, too, Rosa,' Amy whispered back. '*Buon Natale!*'

Happy Christmas!

'*Buon Natale, Nonna.*' Amy helped her grandmother into the chair she had been sleeping in.

'*Buon Natale, Mamma.*'

But Marcella wasn't listening. Ignoring all the monitors, the IV lines, the beeping noises and everything else alarming, she was leaning over the bed, gently touching Summer's face, murmuring a constant stream of endearments.

'*Oh!*' Amy clutched her sister's hand and spoke in a hushed voice, not wanting to break the spell. 'Rosa, *look*! Summer's waking up.'

And she was.

Slowly. Peacefully. Surrounded by the voices and touch of the three women who were all mothers to her. Watched over by a benevolent small figure who sat, imperiously, in the armchair nodding and muttering approvingly at regular intervals.

Staff came and went unobtrusively, keeping a close watch on what was happening but not disturbing this special family moment.

Luke was there. He smiled at Amy. A smile that told her

he understood how special this was. That he understood how much this mattered.

Amy smiled back. Including him. Pulling him in to share the magic. Trying to find and reach through that crack she knew was there. To reach inside Luke—so he wouldn't feel lonely.

To let him know he never needed to feel lonely again.

The smile went on. And on.

It was no wonder Rosa noticed. She looked from Amy to Luke and back again. Then she stepped to where Luke was standing, well back from the end of Summer's bed.

'Does it hurt?' she queried. 'Where her chest was cut open for the operation?'

'Surprisingly little,' Luke responded. 'Pain from fractures comes from movement and there's very little movement of the sternum involved in breathing. Most children can be discharged from open-heart surgery with nothing more than paracetamol needed to relieve any discomfort. You'll be amazed at how soon Summer's up and about.'

Rosa had been listening carefully. Watching and assessing Luke just as carefully. She gave Amy a quick grin as she stepped back towards her sister.

'E un bell 'uomo, vero?'

Amy just raised her eyebrows. This was hardly the place to talk about how good-looking Luke was. Just as well he didn't speak Italian, wasn't it?

There was just a hint of a wink in Luke's expression as he nodded at Rosa while moving away, however.

'Grazie,' he murmured.

Nonna scowled disapprovingly. Rosa's jaw dropped and she flushed bright pink. Amy shut her eyes for a moment, took a deep breath and then walked after Luke, but he was now standing beside the ICU consultant so she could hardly apologise for her sister's inappropriate comment.

'Summer needs to rest,' the consultant reminded Amy. 'It's great if she has one or possibly two of you with her at all times, but we can't have this many here all day.'

'And it's Christmas,' Luke added. 'You'll all want some time with the other children, yes?'

Amy nodded.

'Henry's waiting. He'll take you back as soon as you're ready.'

'Rosa will want to see the twins,' Amy thought aloud. 'And Nonna will need a rest after travelling. I'll talk to Mamma. I can stay if she wants to see the others.'

Luke frowned, as though that plan wasn't the best. But then he simply nodded. 'Let me know,' he said, a little curtly. 'I have to go myself. I have a few things that need attention.' He turned back to the ICU consultant. 'I've got my mobile, of course,' he said, 'but I'd prefer not to be called unless it's an emergency.'

The consultant smiled. 'Of course. Enjoy your Christmas, Luke. Things are looking good here. You're happy with the lad you were working on last night?'

Luke nodded. 'Poor kid. Getting caught up in a gang fight and shot on Christmas Eve was a bit rough. He lost a lot of blood but I'm happy his cardiac function will remain normal. What we need to watch is...'

His voice faded into the background as Amy went back to her family. So Henry was taking them back to the manor and Luke had things that needed his attention. Was he not planning to go home for Christmas? Some of the shine of happiness from Summer's waking up and the reunion with her family faded.

Marcella elected to stay.

'I'll come and see the rest of my *bambina* later,' she said firmly. 'Right now, it's this little *angelo* that needs me the most.'

'We'll take Nonna with us, then,' Rosa said. 'Come on, Amy. I can't wait to see the boys.' She took her turn to kiss Summer. 'See you later, *tesora*.'

Summer smiled and gave an infinitesimal nod, but her gaze went straight back to Marcella.

'Mamma,' she whispered.

'I'm here, *carina*. I'm staying right beside you.'

'Chiesa!'

'It's a chapel, Nonna. A small church.' Amy hadn't seen the beautiful stone structure in the dark last night, but this morning, with its roof and the tops of surrounding gravestones softly blanketed by the deep snow, it was clearly visible amidst a forest of huge tree trunks.

Her grandmother crossed herself and nodded approvingly. *'Buona.'*

She approved of the Harrington family's faith. What would she say when she learned the Italian connection with a woman who lay buried in that small private cemetery? There was no way she would approve of a broken family. A father who had been deprived of his only child. Maybe it was just as well she spoke only her native language.

Rosa was still getting her head around the astonishing information Amy had shared—in English—during their journey from the city.

'It's so weird! Uncle Vanni's son? And you've been working with him for so long and we never knew. Who'd have thought?'

'He keeps his background very private.'

'I can see why.' Rosa was gaping as the manor house came into view. 'It's like something out of a fairy tale. If people knew how rich he was, he'd be beating women off with a stick.' She eyed her sister. 'He's not beating you off, from what I could see.'

'I'm not after his money,' Amy said sadly. 'If anything, I wish he didn't have a background like this. It makes things impossible. Wait till you meet his grandmother. She hates me so much she couldn't bear to stay in the same room as me last night.'

'Because you're in love with her grandson?'

'We haven't got that far. I think she hates me because I'm half-Italian. And because I'm connected with Uncle Vanni. I remind her of how she lost her daughter.'

They were parking in front of the house now. 'I saved that scrapbook,' she told Rosa. 'It might be the only thing of Uncle Vanni's that isn't lost in the fire. I'd been carrying it in my bag to show Luke and I'd forgotten all about it,'

Which had been hardly surprising because that had been when she'd been swept off her feet. Made love to with a passion that had driven all else from her mind. And from there she had been whirled into a series of unexpected and very sharp turns in her life.

'I left it outside Lady Harrington's bedroom door last night when I went back to be with Summer. I wonder if she's even looked at it?'

There was no sign of Lady Harrington when Elaine met them at the front door.

'We're all in the kitchen,' she told Amy, 'having our Christmas breakfast.'

Nonna seemed to be overcome by the sight of the Christmas tree in the foyer. Amy took her arm and urged her gently forward.

'It's just the Christmas tree, Nonna,' she said reassuringly. '*Albero di Natale*. Isn't it beautiful?'

Nonna made a clucking sound that said, very eloquently, that she disapproved of such opulence, but she followed Amy and Rosa willingly enough.

'I've made a room ready for your nanna,' Elaine said to Amy. 'She'll need to rest, I expect.'

'Soon,' Amy agreed.

'Where's Lady Harrington?' Rosa queried politely. 'I should introduce myself.'

Elaine looked embarrassed. 'I expect she'll be down soon.'

Christmas morning with six children in a house should have been seething with excitement, but the atmosphere in the huge, old kitchen was very solemn until Marco and Angelo spotted their mother.

'*Mamma!*' They scrambled from their seats at the table and launched themselves in Rosa's direction like small, human torpedoes.

Elaine laughed. The cook, Beryl, wiped her hands on her apron and grinned. Monty got up from his blanket in the corner to see what the fuss was all about. The other children, however, stayed at the table. They had plates of food in front of them. Slices of crusty bread and butter that looked homemade. Bacon and eggs and tiny sausages beside baked beans and mushrooms and potato cakes. The sort of food that was a special treat but they didn't seem to be eating much of it.

When the initial excitement of Rosa's arrival subsided, they all sent wary glances towards Nonna, who was now sitting at the far end of the table, and then went back to playing with their food.

'What's the matter?' Amy finally asked. 'Aren't you happy Summer's OK? You'll all be able to visit her in a day or two. Only one at a time, but I think she'll be home again before very long.'

That did it. Robert pushed his plate away, his fork clattering onto the china.

'We haven't *got* a home any more,' he said sullenly. 'It got burned, didn't it?'

'Not all of it. We'll fix things,' Amy promised.

'No, we won't. And even if we do, your Mr Harrington's going to take it away from us, so what's the point?'

Elaine exchanged a glance with Beryl. Raised eyebrows and quick head shakes indicated they knew nothing about this.

'And…' Quiet Andrew was looking as miserable as Robert. 'It's Christmas!'

Chantelle burst into tears. 'And we haven't got any presents,' she sobbed. 'Not even *one!*'

Amy sent a desperate glance towards Rosa, but her sister looked stricken. Maybe the credit card hadn't been robust enough to deal with any airport shopping.

'Hey!' Amy gathered Chantelle into her arms, taking her chair and smiling at the rest of the children. 'We've got each other, haven't we? We're all safe and we're all together. That's what *really* matters.' She waited until Robert raised his head and caught her gaze. 'Nobody is going to take our house away. Nobody.' She hugged Chantelle. 'And Summer got a present, didn't she? The best present she could ever get. A new heart.'

'So she's not going to die?' Robert's Adam's apple bobbed and his voice cracked and rose.

'She's got every chance of living now,' Amy said confidently. 'Much, much more than she had a couple of days ago.'

'And Monty's OK,' she went on, trying to put a positive spin on this strange Christmas Day. 'And he's like a present, too, isn't he? He can't live with Zoe and her mum any more so he's our pet.'

'Really?' Rosa reached past the twins to stroke the huge dog. 'Cool!'

Elaine put a steaming cup of tea in front of Nonna.

'Grazie,' the old woman said.

Elaine patted her hand. 'You're welcome, Nanna.'

Beryl filled the kettle again. 'Your Henry's coming back from putting the car away. He'll be wanting some breakfast.'

She didn't take the kettle away from beneath the tap, however. She was still intent on peering out the window.

'Mercy!' she said, as cold water flowed over the top of the kettle and then her hand. She abandoned the tea-making and peered from the window again. 'I don't believe this,' she muttered.

'What?' Elaine joined her at the sink. 'Oh, *my!*' She flapped a hand in a beckoning gesture. 'Children! You'd better come and see. Quick! Out the front.'

The excitement was contagious. A small stampede of children followed, Elaine with Rosa and twins bringing up the rear, closely followed by Monty who gave a single, loud woof as he bounded through the kitchen door.

Amy looked at Nonna but she was sipping her tea, apparently unperturbed.

'I'll stay with your granny,' Beryl offered. 'You go and see.'

Amy went.

CHAPTER TWELVE

By the time Amy reached the foyer, the front door was wide open and sparkling, cold air was pouring into the house.

The sound of bells could be heard, getting louder and louder.

Amy reached the door. The children were all standing on the top step, a semicircle of faces that all had open mouths and wide eyes.

And no wonder!

Coming down the long driveway, covered in tinsel, was a small lorry. The shop name 'Barkers' could be seen beneath loops of tinsel, painted in old-fashioned lettering on the side, but it was no ordinary shop employee that climbed down from the driver's seat.

He was wearing a red suit with white trim and he had ridiculously bushy eyebrows and a fluffy white beard that reached his chest.

'Ho, ho, ho,' he boomed. 'Merry Christmas!'

He winked at the adults. 'Sorry, I'm late. Lots of snow on the M1 last night.'

His gaze rested for just a fraction of a second on Amy.

Just long enough for her to know who was beneath the pillow stomach and bushy eyebrows.

Luca!

It was understandable that Rosa and the children didn't recognise him, but Elaine seemed just as taken in. Because doing something like this was so out of character for the Harrington grandson and heir?

The back door of the lorry was folding down, the recorded bells still jingling merrily.

'Come,' Father Christmas invited the children. 'Come and see what I've got.'

The children moved slowly down the steps. They stood in the driveway, staring into the back of the lorry, and the adults were not far behind.

'Oh, my!' Elaine breathed.

Amy blinked. And blinked again. The back of this lorry was full of brightly wrapped parcels. Hundreds of them, it seemed.

'I forgot my sack,' Father Christmas said. 'Can someone show me where the tree is and give me a hand to get them all inside?'

Robert stepped forward and spoke in a steady, deep voice. 'I can do that.'

The noise could have woken the dead.

Happy shouting. Laughter. Squeals of glee.

The gifts were amazing. Someone—possibly many people—had been given a list of those involved. Their ages and approximate sizes and the information that they had lost most of their belongings.

Many of the first packages contained clothes. Jeans and T-shirts and warm, fleecy jackets. Anoraks and gumboots in wonderful bright colours. Kyra's were pink with lime-green spots.

'Wow!' she said. 'These are *way* cool!'

Henry and Elaine and Beryl watched from the library door. Amy sat on the stairs, brushing tears form her cheeks on more than one occasion. Totally unable to wipe the smile from her face.

She was riveted by the scene. The generosity was overwhelming and the joy of the children heart-warming, but the real magic came from watching this Father Christmas. The joy *he* was getting, acting the part. Using Robert as his right-hand man.

'You're the chief elf!' he boomed in that astonishingly deep, unrecognisable voice. 'You get to find the next gift.'

Robert was scrupulously fair, making sure everyone had their turns.

It was Chantelle who pointed out when Robert was due for a gift. She tugged shyly at Santa's sleeve.

'It wouldn't be fair, would it? If the chief elf got left out?'

'You can be the deputy chief elf,' Luke told her. 'You get to find a present for Robert.'

'How did you know all our names?'

'I'm Father Christmas! I know everybody's names.'

Chantelle sighed happily. 'I love you, Santa.'

'I love you, too, chicken.'

Amy's joy overflowed and she gurgled with laughter. Father Christmas looked up and she knew *he* knew that she had recognised him. It was their secret and Amy could barely tear her gaze away from him as the gift distribution continued. She was waiting for each moment of connection.

Loving him more each time.

At one point she had to look up to blink away more tears and it was then that she saw the solitary figure standing to one side of the U at the top of the stairs, gripping the banister with one hand.

Lady Prudence Harrington looked dishevelled. She wore a dressing-gown and her hair was unbrushed. She didn't·see Amy's shocked glance. She was too intent on watching her grandson and the children.

Amy saw something else, as well. Clutched beneath the old woman's arm was the leather-bound scrapbook of Caroline's. The knowledge that her gift had been accepted only added to the magic. Amy turned back to keep watching the seemingly endless stream of gifts.

There were toys galore. Lovely toys, like Lego for the twins and Meccano for Andrew. Robert had a telescope and books about astronomy. There were soft toy animals for Chantelle and a hair straightener and make-up for Kyra. There were even toys for Monty. A Frisbee and flinger. Rawhide treats and a huge, soft bed.

Rosa received perfume and chocolates and there was a beautiful mohair knee rug for Nonna. Parcels were put aside for Marcella and Summer. The massive pile of gifts was finally whittled down and the deputy elf tugged on Santa's sleeve again, this time with more urgency.

'But what about *Amy*?' she demanded. 'Where's *her* present?'

'Ah!' Luke's voice was still deep but it softened. 'I have a very special present for Amy. It's outside.'

Amy caught her breath. What could it be? Robert looked up from one of his books. 'Can we come and see it?'

Father Christmas shook his head. 'I'm afraid not.'

'Why not?' Chantelle asked. 'We *love* Amy.'

'I know, chicken. So do I.'

A sensation as though a bottle of champagne had been opened inside Amy sent its fizz right through her body. He loved her?

Chantelle seemed just as amazed. *'Really?'* But then she nodded. 'Because you love everybody, right?'

'Yes. But *especially* Amy.' He was looking directly at her and Amy couldn't breathe. Couldn't move.

'But why can't we see her present?' Robert took charge of the argument.

'It's not here.'

'You said it was outside!'

'Come,' Father Christmas ordered. 'You'll see what I mean.'

He disappeared into the back of the lorry and there was the sound of an engine roaring into life.

Amy had been able to move after all. She stood with everybody else on the steps and was just as astonished to see Father Christmas emerge, driving carefully down the ramp on a two-seated snowmobile. He did a slow turn and then parked in front of the steps. His gaze was on Amy and she could tell he was smiling beneath the bushy beard because of the way his eyes crinkled.

'Buon Natale,' Father Christmas said in perfect Italian. He patted the seat beside him. *'Vieni con me?'*

Of course Amy would go with him.

Anywhere.

A ride into a blindingly white Christmas day, on a modern sleigh, wrapped in a faux fur blanket with one of Luke's arms around her shoulders was too dreamlike to believe.

They went through a gate and up the long, gentle slope of a hill. At the top of the hill were some huge rocks, jumbled together like a pile of reject material from Stonehenge. A gap between two rocks formed an arch and it was beneath this that Luke parked.

He switched off the machine's motor so that all around them was that peculiar kind of silence a snow-clad landscape could produce, where the sounds of ordinary life were muffled and irrelevant.

'Look,' Luke pointed. 'That's Harrington village.'

Spread below them like a picture on a Christmas card was a church spire and a cluster of cottages. Amy could see the village green, a picturesque pub and a huddle of small shops. To one side of the village, buffered by woods and snow-covered fields, lay Harrington Manor. Smoke curled invitingly from more than one chimney. Somewhere in there were a group of children who were having the most exciting Christmas morning ever.

'Thank you, Luca,' she said softly. 'What you did this morning was amazing. I can't believe you've gone to so much trouble for us. You'd already done enough, you know—giving us a place to stay.'

'Enough? I've barely started.'

Amy caught her breath. Could he mean what she thought he might mean? What she could dream he might mean?

'Did you like it?' Luke held her gaze.

Amy couldn't smile because it was too big. 'It was a whole collection of those moments,' she said solemnly.

'The ones that take your breath away?'

'I felt as if I might never breathe again.'

Luke pulled his hat off, which got rid of the bushy eyebrows. Then he tugged his beard away and, looking like the man Amy had fallen in love with again, he placed a soft kiss on her lips. *'Buono,'* he murmured.

Amy pulled back so she could see his face properly. 'Since when did you start speaking Italian, Mr Harrington?'

In response he pulled her closer so that she was tucked into the circle of his arms. Cushioned on that ridiculous stomach. He kissed her hair but then raised his head to gaze at the scene below them.

'I grew up with this,' he told her. 'My heritage. I used to come up here when I was a boy and look down at everything. It all had my name on it. Harrington village. Harrington school. Even the Harrington Arms. It felt as if the whole world belonged to me and yet I felt...'

Amy twisted a little to look up. 'Lonely?'

'Yes. Not that I understood it then, but I knew something was missing. I thought it was because I was an orphan, except I knew I wasn't. I had a father who didn't want me.'

Not true, but he hadn't known that, had he? Amy slipped her arms over the top of Luke's and pressed so that he was holding her more tightly.

'I felt I deserved to be alone,' Luke said quietly. 'That there was something about me that meant I would always be alone.'

Amy had to swallow the lump in her throat. 'You're not alone, Luca. I'm here.'

'Yes.' He pressed his lips to her hair again and held her so closely it became another moment that took Amy's breath away. 'I don't want to let you go,' he confessed.

'I don't want you to let me go,' Amy responded. 'I love you, Luca Moretti.'

The sound Luke made was almost a groan. 'That's it,' he murmured. 'You turned my world inside out, Amy Phillips. Made me wonder who I actually was. You found the part of me that I knew was missing but could never identify. No...' His voice caught. 'You *are* the part of me that was missing.'

'The Italian half?'

Luke shook his head. 'Not entirely. It goes deeper than

that. Do you remember what you said to me that first night we talked? When I said I intended demolishing the house?'

Amy could feel her cheeks flush. 'I wasn't very polite, was I?'

'You said, "over my dead body" and I was shocked because you meant it. You were prepared to fight for what you were passionate about. To do anything.'

Amy was silent. Embarrassed. Had he really thought that was why she had gone to bed with him?

'I couldn't think of anything I could ever feel like that about,' Luke continued softly. 'Something I would be prepared to lay my life on the line for because life wouldn't be worth living without it. Until...' He drew in a long breath. 'Until I made love to you, Amy. Until I lay there in your arms and felt as though I would never feel lonely again. I know it's far too soon, but I love you. *Ti amo, Amy. Amore mio. Per sempre.* Is that "for ever"? My Italian is more than rusty.'

'I love you, too, Luca.' Amy blinked back her tears. 'It's not too soon and for ever sounds perfect to me, however you say it.'

'Are you sure?'

'I was sure the moment you gave me that box of old Christmas decorations.'

Luke kissed her again. Slowly. With infinite tenderness.

'And I was sure that first time you smiled at me.'

'When was that?'

'When I went along with that lie. When you said I'd come to the house to see how Summer was because I was her doctor. When you were protecting the other children.'

Amy grinned. 'You didn't act like you were in love with me.'

'I just hadn't realised it. I didn't understand what was happening to me. I do now.'

'I'm not sure I do.' Amy wrapped her arms around Luca's neck and brought her face close enough to kiss him. The tip of her nose touched his. 'But maybe I don't need to because it's magic. Christmas magic.'

'No.' His nose moved beneath hers as he shook his head. 'This magic is going to last a lifetime. So many Christmases you won't be able to count them, and every one of them will be magic.'

Amy could feel his breath on her lips and she closed her eyes as she waited for his kiss.

'Just like this,' she murmured.

'Always.'

Hours later. Many hours later, Luke was kissing Amy yet again. This time in the comfort of the glow the library fire was providing.

The house was almost as quiet as the hilltop had been because everyone else had long since gone to bed.

'This has been the most amazing day of my life,' Amy said, when she had a moment to catch her breath. 'Thank you.'

'What for?'

'For everything.' Amy started to count the reasons off on her fingers. 'For saving Summer and giving her a new chance of life. For bringing the children here. For that extraordinary pile of presents. For the Christmas dinner and having Mr Battersby here with those papers that gave the house to Mamma. For...*this*!' Amy held up her left hand.

Luke groaned. 'You're not supposed to be wearing that. It came out of a Christmas cracker, for heaven's sake. It's rubbish!'

It was. A lurid, square, pink stone stuck to a gaudy gold band, but Luke had offered it to her. In front of everybody, and it had been his choice to slip it onto the third finger of her left hand. Nobody had missed the significance of that gesture and the fabulous meal had become a celebration of far more than Christmas.

'I'm wearing it,' Amy said stubbornly.

'I'm replacing it, then,' Luke said firmly. 'With the real thing. As soon as the shops are open again. In fact, I'm sure Mr Barker wouldn't mind doing me one more small favour and I believe they have a wonderful selection of jewellery. I'll talk to him tomorrow.'

Amy sighed with contentment and gave herself up to another one of those kisses she would never, ever tire of. The clock in the corner was reminding them that the last minutes of this Christmas day might be ticking away but there still seemed to be plenty of magic in the air.

It was Luke who spoke when they reluctantly drew apart.

'It's me who should be thanking you,' he said.

'What for?'

'For giving my grandmother that scrapbook. I don't think she's ever going to put it down. She says she feels as if you've given her back part of her daughter. The happiest part.'

'Did you hear her say *"Buon Natale"* to Nonna?'

'Yes.' Luke smiled. 'Her accent was atrocious but it's a start, isn't it?' He held Amy close. 'You've changed everything for us, my love. Especially for me. I don't think I can ever tell you how grateful I am that I've found you. That, by some extraordinary miracle, you love me. It's too new. Too wonderful.'

'It's real,' Amy assured him. 'And this is my gift to you today, Luca. My love. My heart and soul. For ever.'

Luca's eyes were suspiciously bright. 'Then it's the same as my gift to you. *Buon Natale*, Amy.'

'*Buon Natale*, Luca.'

MILLS & BOON®
Pure reading pleasure™

OCTOBER 2008 HARDBACK TITLES

ROMANCE

The Greek Tycoon's Disobedient Bride *Lynne Graham*	978 0 263 20366 0
The Venetian's Midnight Mistress *Carole Mortimer*	978 0 263 20367 7
Ruthless Tycoon, Innocent Wife *Helen Brooks*	978 0 263 20368 4
The Sheikh's Wayward Wife *Sandra Marton*	978 0 263 20369 1
The Fiorenza Forced Marriage *Melanie Milburne*	978 0 263 20370 7
The Spanish Billionaire's Christmas Bride *Maggie Cox*	978 0 263 20371 4
The Ruthless Italian's Inexperienced Wife *Christina Hollis*	978 0 263 20372 1
Claimed for the Italian's Revenge *Natalie Rivers*	978 0 263 20373 8
The Italian's Christmas Miracle *Lucy Gordon*	978 0 263 20374 5
Cinderella and the Cowboy *Judy Christenberry*	978 0 263 20375 2
His Mistletoe Bride *Cara Colter*	978 0 263 20376 9
Pregnant: Father Wanted *Claire Baxter*	978 0 263 20377 6
Marry-Me Christmas *Shirley Jump*	978 0 263 20378 3
Her Baby's First Christmas *Susan Meier*	978 0 263 20379 0
One Magical Christmas *Carol Marinelli*	978 0 263 20380 6
The GP's Meant-To-Be Bride *Jennifer Taylor*	978 0 263 20381 3

HISTORICAL

Miss Winbolt and the Fortune Hunter *Sylvia Andrew*	978 0 263 20213 7
Captain Fawley's Innocent Bride *Annie Burrows*	978 0 263 20214 4
The Rake's Rebellious Lady *Anne Herries*	978 0 263 20215 1

MEDICAL™

A Mummy for Christmas *Caroline Anderson*	978 0 263 19914 7
A Bride and Child Worth Waiting For *Marion Lennox*	978 0 263 19915 4
The Italian Surgeon's Christmas Miracle *Alison Roberts*	978 0 263 19916 1
Children's Doctor, Christmas Bride *Lucy Clark*	978 0 263 19917 8

MILLS & BOON®

Pure reading pleasure™

OCTOBER 2008 LARGE PRINT TITLES

ROMANCE

The Sheikh's Blackmailed Mistress *Penny Jordan*	978 0 263 20082 9
The Millionaire's Inexperienced Love-Slave *Miranda Lee*	978 0 263 20083 6
Bought: The Greek's Innocent Virgin *Sarah Morgan*	978 0 263 20084 3
Bedded at the Billionaire's Convenience *Cathy Williams*	978 0 263 20085 0
The Pregnancy Promise *Barbara McMahon*	978 0 263 20086 7
The Italian's Cinderella Bride *Lucy Gordon*	978 0 263 20087 4
Saying Yes to the Millionaire *Fiona Harper*	978 0 263 20088 1
Her Royal Wedding Wish *Cara Colter*	978 0 263 20089 8

HISTORICAL

Untouched Mistress *Margaret McPhee*	978 0 263 20169 7
A Less Than Perfect Lady *Elizabeth Beacon*	978 0 263 20170 3
Viking Warrior, Unwilling Wife *Michelle Styles*	978 0 263 20171 0

MEDICAL™

The Doctor's Royal Love-Child *Kate Hardy*	978 0 263 19980 2
His Island Bride *Marion Lennox*	978 0 263 19981 9
A Consultant Beyond Compare *Joanna Neil*	978 0 263 19982 6
The Surgeon Boss's Bride *Melanie Milburne*	978 0 263 19983 3
A Wife Worth Waiting For *Maggie Kingsley*	978 0 263 19984 0
Desert Prince, Expectant Mother *Olivia Gates*	978 0 263 19985 7

MILLS & BOON®
Pure reading pleasure™

NOVEMBER 2008 HARDBACK TITLES

ROMANCE

The Billionaire's Bride of Vengeance *Miranda Lee*	978 0 263 20382 0
The Santangeli Marriage *Sara Craven*	978 0 263 20383 7
The Spaniard's Virgin Housekeeper *Diana Hamilton*	978 0 263 20384 4
The Greek Tycoon's Reluctant Bride *Kate Hewitt*	978 0 263 20385 1
Innocent Mistress, Royal Wife *Robyn Donald*	978 0 263 20386 8
Taken for Revenge, Bedded for Pleasure *India Grey*	978 0 263 20387 5
The Billionaire Boss's Innocent Bride *Lindsay Armstrong*	978 0 263 20388 2
The Billionaire's Defiant Wife *Amanda Browning*	978 0 263 20389 9
Nanny to the Billionaire's Son *Barbara McMahon*	978 0 263 20390 5
Cinderella and the Sheikh *Natasha Oakley*	978 0 263 20391 2
Promoted: Secretary to Bride! *Jennie Adams*	978 0 263 20392 9
The Black Sheep's Proposal *Patricia Thayer*	978 0 263 20393 6
The Snow-Kissed Bride *Linda Goodnight*	978 0 263 20394 3
The Rancher's Runaway Princess *Donna Alward*	978 0 263 20395 0
The Greek Doctor's New-Year Baby *Kate Hardy*	978 0 263 20396 7
The Wife He's Been Waiting For *Dianne Drake*	978 0 263 20397 4

HISTORICAL

The Captain's Forbidden Miss *Margaret McPhee*	978 0 263 20216 8
The Earl and the Hoyden *Mary Nichols*	978 0 263 20217 5
From Governess to Society Bride *Helen Dickson*	978 0 263 20218 2

MEDICAL™

The Heart Surgeon's Secret Child *Meredith Webber*	978 0 263 19918 5
The Midwife's Little Miracle *Fiona McArthur*	978 0 263 19919 2
The Single Dad's New-Year Bride *Amy Andrews*	978 0 263 19920 8
Posh Doc Claims His Bride *Anne Fraser*	978 0 263 19921 5

MILLS & BOON®
Pure reading pleasure™

NOVEMBER 2008 LARGE PRINT TITLES

ROMANCE

Bought for Revenge, Bedded for Pleasure *Emma Darcy*	978 0 263 20090 4
Forbidden: The Billionaire's Virgin Princess *Lucy Monroe*	978 0 263 20091 1
The Greek Tycoon's Convenient Wife *Sharon Kendrick*	978 0 263 20092 8
The Marciano Love-Child *Melanie Milburne*	978 0 263 20093 5
Parents in Training *Barbara McMahon*	978 0 263 20094 2
Newlyweds of Convenience *Jessica Hart*	978 0 263 20095 9
The Desert Prince's Proposal *Nicola Marsh*	978 0 263 20096 6
Adopted: Outback Baby *Barbara Hannay*	978 0 263 20097 3

HISTORICAL

The Virtuous Courtesan *Mary Brendan*	978 0 263 20172 7
The Homeless Heiress *Anne Herries*	978 0 263 20173 4
Rebel Lady, Convenient Wife *June Francis*	978 0 263 20174 1

MEDICAL™

Nurse Bride, Bayside Wedding *Gill Sanderson*	978 0 263 19986 4
Billionaire Doctor, Ordinary Nurse *Carol Marinelli*	978 0 263 19987 1
The Sheikh Surgeon's Baby *Meredith Webber*	978 0 263 19988 8
The Outback Doctor's Surprise Bride *Amy Andrews*	978 0 263 19989 5
A Wedding at Limestone Coast *Lucy Clark*	978 0 263 19990 1
The Doctor's Meant-To-Be Marriage *Janice Lynn*	978 0 263 19991 8